The Rain, the Park and Other Things

The Rain, the Park and Other Things

Alan C. Williams

The Rain, the Park and Other Things

The Rain, the Park and Other Things
ISBN 978 1 76041 840 3
Copyright © Alan C. Williams 2020
Cover painting © Alan C. Williams 2020

First published 2020 by
GINNINDERRA PRESS
PO Box 3461 Port Adelaide 5015
www.ginninderrapress.com.au

Contents

The Rain, the Park and Other Things

Yesterday was a day when it rained forever. It was absolutely fantastic, sitting outside in my back garden and watching the deluge soaking everything. Of course, that included me but I didn't mind at all. I sat as silver rivulets cascaded from the leaves on to the grass.

I love the rain and I tell it how much all the time. The trouble is the clouds don't always hear my tiny voice. This was the first decent downpour in months.

There's something about the sound of raindrops; as though they're alive. When I'm inside trying to get to sleep, they sound like someone singing a lullaby when they splash against the windows of my home. In some weird way, I imagine that they're talking back to me, describing the adventures that they've experienced in the skies up above.

Yeah, yesterday was definitely great. It was upsetting to hear about the floods in Brisbane on the morning news, especially the part about the predicted five more days of continued deluges. Elsewhere, southern Tasmania was experiencing the worst drought in years with a real danger of a massive failure of the apple industry. Hopefully, things will change soon.

I feel rejuvenated when I start work this morning. I think that I'm ready for anything. And then Miserable Maggie storms up to my desk.

'Where's those figures on the Anderson account, Summers? I need them now!'

'But…but you only asked for them last thing on Tuesday and I was on a flexi-day yesterday,' I stammer. 'I've only just begun to collate them.'

'Not my fault if you take time off. You should have worked late on Tuesday, shouldn't you! Well, shouldn't you?'

I'm about to make a comment about unpaid overtime and perhaps, if she were able to organise herself better, before I remember that I'm on my final warning. I gaze at the floor. 'Yes. I'm sorry, Ms Bedford. I'll do them straight away.'

'Make sure you do, young lady. I want them before I have my hair done at lunchtime.'

'Big date?' I inquire, without thinking.

Her icy stare and shouted comments about minding my own business confirm my guess. Miserable Maggie on a date? I feel sorry for her would-be partner.

After that, the day becomes worse and worse. I work through lunch so that I can leave early. It's begun to rain once more and I know I'll explode if I don't get outside. At least relaxing in the rain showers will help calm me down so I grab my sports bag and literally run across the road to sit on the park bench. Working there with that harridan, Maggie blinking Bedford, is becoming more than I can bear.

The wooden bench's sopping, yet I don't care. I sit down and stare back up at the first-floor offices of Transudes where I work. How many more days can I stay there? Finding another job will be difficult in this uncertain financial climate and there's no one else to support me. No parents, no boyfriend, not even a housemate.

I know that my so-called working colleagues are watching me surreptitiously from their windows, making snide comments about me being here, getting drenched. I don't care. None of them are my friends. At least out here in the open, under the soaking rains, I can be free…I can be me.

I close my eyes and lean back against the bench, stretching my arms to grab the top of the seat on each side. Within moments, I can sense the tension being washed away by the gentle showers. The rain drizzles through my hair, streaming down my face onto my sodden clothing.

Even as a little girl, Mum and Dad were worried about my fixation because I refused to come inside when there was a storm or even a shower. In the end, they accepted it, always making sure I didn't get too cold or sick. Mum used to say that it was cheaper than horse-riding lessons like my sister had and, if it made me happy, then that was okay.

'Just a few more minutes, please. One more cloudburst would be lovely,' I say quietly.

'You look as though you're enjoying yourself, Miss.'

I jump at the voice from in front of me. Rubbing my eyes, I peer up to see a man standing before me. He has an umbrella over his head and is wearing a waterproof coat. I recognise him. He also works in our offices. I've seen him a few times in passing, although I doubt if he's noticed me.

As for his appearance, I reckon he's about ten years older than me, in his mid-thirties. He's a little on the chubby side but these days most of us are. If anything is interesting about him, I would have to say it's his deep blue eyes and his smile. Thinking about it, he looks quite dreamy. I'm pleased that he's here.

'Actually, I'm having a great time.' I reply, nodding towards the large office building. 'At least I don't have to listen to Miserable Maggie wittering on when I'm down here,'

'Your boss? Let me guess. Maggie Bedford? You're in Accounts?'

'Guilty as charged. I'm on my final warning, so don't say anything, please,' I add, realising the nature of office politics. I shuffle forward on the bench. Here I am looking like a drowned rat while talking to a half-decent-looking guy. My long black hair's plastered to my face and paisley blouse.

'I've seen you down here in the park a couple of times. I only started at Transudes recently and I was intrigued. Thought you might like some company.'

'What? Sitting in the rain?'

He nods.

'Okay…but only if you put the umbrella down, take off that coat and share the experience,' I dare him.

'Fair enough! By the way, my name's Tony. Tony Peterson. Yours?'

'Yvonne.' I watch as he closes the umbrella, doffs his jacket before gingerly sitting down on my left. He winces as the pools of cool water on the seat soak into his slacks. At the same time, it begins to pour down more heavily and within minutes he's as saturated as I. We stare at the state of one another and simultaneously burst into laughter. Anyone passing by would think that we're mad.

'When I came down here, I thought you were talking to someone. Mind if I ask who?'

'The rain.'

'And…does it answer you?'

'Don't be daft. However, it is a great listener. I was…no, it doesn't matter. You probably think I'm barking already, sitting out here.'

We remain there in silence for a few minutes.

'I bet you were a splasher when you were a boy,' I eventually say to him.

'Beg your pardon?' he replies, leaning towards me to be heard.

'A splasher! If you saw a puddle did you jump into it or were you a walk-arounder?'

'Oh, definitely a splasher! Funny. I'd forgotten that. Nowadays I'm more of a very cautious walk-arounder unfortunately, avoiding awkward situations. I'm probably too cautious.'

'Well, I'm still always jumping in, feet first. Gets me into trouble but a leopard can't change her stripes, can she?'

Tony's about to correct my mixed metaphor but sees my wry smile. I continue. 'What you need is someone to remind you to take a chance now and then.'

'Someone like you?'

'Why not? That's why you came over to see me just now. Every other guy in the office avoids me like the bubonic plague but you crossed that line. Now your reputation is shot. No one will talk to you. Can't you see them all watching us from up there, safe and snug, behind their windows?'

Tony looks up, peering through the misty rain to the grey concrete walls of our workplace building. 'I doubt that, Yvonne. And if they do, they won't dare say anything to my face. I'm in charge of the News team.'

'The News? Does that include the Weather, too?'

'Oh yes, the Weather… Actually, I've been considering a new angle to that. It seems to me that the presenters are all the same, almost like clones. I need our channel to stand out from the others. A new gimmick…or approach?'

'Whatever do you mean?' I ask.

'I'm not sure…I don't know…possibly a presenter who embraces rainy weather for a change. After all, we live in a country where rain is a welcome and precious resource but usually all you see is some person, huddled under an umbrella, apologising for the wet. That doesn't make sense to me. Think about it! There's lots of farmers, gardeners out there too, even people who want a nice, green lawn instead of a dried-out mess of dandelions. We've been ignoring them and what they might desire.'

His imagination's kicking in now and, despite being wet, he's grinning. 'Yes…that's exactly who I'm searching for. I can see her now; it's got to be a woman. People trust women more. "Sorry folks. I've got some bad news for you today; another stinking, horrible day of sunshine. Don't worry, though. It's going to be much better on Thursday – torrential rain all over. A chance to get those wellies out… or better still take them off and have a splash in your bare feet."'

He leans back on the bench, puzzled. 'Now…that's strange. Half an hour ago, I was considering which direction to take with the programme. I notice you out here in the rain again, I talk to you and suddenly I realise exactly what I need.'

He stares at me. Raindrops run down his forehead and drip from his eyelashes and his nose. As for me, I try to maintain a blank expression on my face. It's difficult.

'Look at you, Yvonne. You love these showers. You're not afraid to get your feet wet, are you? Come on! Get up and tell me all about this weather.'

'What? Like a weather reporter?' I ask.

Tony nods. So I kick off my shoes, walk forward and pretend I'm telling people about this rainy day. All the time, I'm chatting about clouds and rainbows while stamping around then kicking my toes through the puddles. Truthfully, I don't have to act. I do what I love to do. Nevertheless, next time I dance around like this, I should avoid wearing a dress. Some of those splashes…

He claps as I take a bow. 'That was brilliant. I loved it. You're a natural. Exactly the person that I need.'

Tony suggests returning to the studios and inquires how I'd feel about a new job as a weather girl on television. I'm ecstatic. I never liked Accounts and now…? The chance to be me; telling other people about what's going to happen up in the skies…? It'll be perfect.

I tell him how wonderful it will be and isn't it a fantastic coincidence that we met just when he was searching for a new approach. He agrees.

Actually, I heard about his plans to revamp the weather and it isn't happenstance that my park bench is directly across the road from his office window. I'd read once about self-fulfilling prophecies; that if you want something to happen strongly enough then it will come true. Nevertheless, there's nothing wrong with giving fate a helping hand, is there?

'Coming?' Tony asks as he begins to wander back. 'By the way, I don't even know your full name.'

'It's Summers. Yvonne Summers.'

'How appropriate…for a weather girl, I mean. We need to do some paperwork to transfer you from Accounts. And sort you out with a wardrobe for tomorrow. And…if you're free this evening, maybe…we could…grab a bite to eat?' He's blushing.

'I did miss out on lunch…so, dinner? Yeah. That sounds great. Need to change my clothes, though. You should too.'

He wrings some water out of his jacket and we make our way down the pathway toward Transudes.

*

Over the years since my childhood, I discovered that I have a special gift. It's one that I'll be able to use even more when I'm presenting weather reports to the Aussie people. The climate has been causing havoc and disrupting society in our country for far too long.

Tomorrow, the droughts will finish when much-needed rains come to apple-growing areas of Tassie. Elsewhere, the torrential downpours around Brisbane will mysteriously cease.

I'm certain of it.

After all, I'm a Rain Whisperer.

Normally I can only talk to the clouds nearby but tomorrow, tens of thousands of television sets tuned into my weather forecasts will whisper to the clouds above them.

They'll be simple instructions, spoken so softly that the people watching will never notice but the clouds will hear them; every single word!

'Rain!' I'll ask the wispy clouds around the Huon Valley, south-west of Hobart or I'll suggest 'Don't rain!' to the smoke-grey cumulonimbus clouds over southern Queensland. And the clouds will listen then obey.

*

I'm jolted back to reality when Tony asks me to hold hands with him. The showers have stopped. Now the evening sun is breaking through the pink-tinged clouds.

'That's a bit forward of you, Mr Peterson,' I protest, coquettishly.

Tony's childlike face grins back at mine. 'One last puddle? Together?' he suggests.

I clasp his hand then we jump. Water splashes everywhere.

We're still laughing when I notice Maggie leaving the building. She's obviously had her hair styled. In addition, she's wearing a fetching, new two-piece suit.

'See that lady in the red over there?' I indicate, to no one in particular. 'An itsy-bitsy shower above her would make my day perfect. Just a few drops, mind you.'

Maggie's surprised cry a few moments later causes Tony to turn his head as he crosses the street. Me, I don't bother looking, although I do say a quiet 'Thank you' to my friends. Even though I'm taking on the responsibility of secretly influencing Australia's weather for the foreseeable future, I'm sure that it's all right to have a little fun along the way.

The Rain

Tourist

We've been busy today and I'm not complaining. Now we have some more visitors…more tourists in search of souvenirs.

He's wearing one of those tasteless Hawaiian shirts and carrying a video camera in his hand. She's wearing sunglasses although it's dark and pouring down outside.

'Decent-looking shop you have.' He's talking to me.

'Thank you,' I say, politely. Foreign tourists, especially the long- haul ones, don't tend to spend as much due to restrictions on baggage weight. These ones are Americans…or possibly Canadians. I can never tell.

'We're tourists,' he says, almost proudly.

I give him one of my friendly smiles. They're Americans. No doubt about it.

'So, where else are you off to…besides here?' I notice that Lynda, my young assistant, is helping Mrs Tourist to choose a scarf. After all, scarves are light and don't take up much room.

'Wine Glass Bay. It's on our list of must-sees. Have you been there?'

'Oh yes. It's well worth a visit. Might I suggest that you have a wander along the beach at Coles Bay on the way. The way that clouds form over the Hazards mountains is stunning.'

'Thanks. We probably won't have time. "Schedule" you understand.'

'Yes, of course. Schedule.'

He wanders over to chat to his wife. Lynda will look after them now.

I relax, recalling my first visit to Freycinet with my wife. It wasn't that long ago and my life had certainly changed since then. The

American has a schedule, same as Robyn. She loved her schedules so much. Let's see…when were we there? August? Yes, late August.

*

'Come on, Robyn. Let's w-wander down here for a…a bit. We can check out the coast and those…those mountains there. See how tho-those clouds appear and disappear? Be-besides. It'll be g-good to stretch our legs. We've been dri-driving all day and… Robyn, what are you do-doing?'

'We're going back to the car. We've seen Freycinet. Time to move on. I'll drive. You're too slow. We've got to get to Bicheno before three.'

'Why? Can't we st-stay here and walk…'

'What? To l-l-look at fluffy clouds? You really are thick, aren't you, Davey.'

I hate it when she calls me that, although I've given up telling her. My name's Dave or David. I wouldn't say she deliberately does it to irritate me. It's simpl– well, she doesn't think.

'Come on, little Davey,' she says, before looking around, then punching me in the kidneys. It hurts. The previous bruises haven't healed. I try not to show her that I'm in pain as I pick up our shopping bags. She's already walking away.

'Whoops!' she exclaims. 'Almost forgot. Souvenir shop.'

I follow her, reluctantly, predictably; her obedient lapdog. Why do I let her ruin my life? I'm sure I…well, I think I deserve better. To be honest, I've never been sure of anything. Maybe I don't deserve more than this…

'Do you sell leather bookmarks?' That's what she'll say next, in that squeaky voice which I've begun to hate.

'Do you have leather bookmarks for sale?' followed by excited squeal number three when the assistant shows her the selection.

There's no doubt about it: my wife is an obsessive, compulsive bookmark collector.

'If you haven't got a bookmark, then no one knows if you've been there,' she tells the young girl.

The assistant smiles back, not having heard Robyn say the same thing to eighty-seven other bookmark sales people. Eighty-seven bloody coloured leather rectangles with embossed pictures and words, proudly displayed in our living room.

I follow her back to the car, opening the passenger door for myself.

'Ahem, Davey. Aren't we forgetting something?'

I stammer an apology in my most subservient tone, rushing to open the driver's door for her. I wait until she's seated, before gently closing it.

'Beautiful women deserve to always be treated with courtesy,' she reminds me with her cold stare. Robyn-Rule, number thirteen.

That evening, back at the caravan that we rented for our four-day break, we examine her two bookmarks from today and the two from our previous day's sightseeing. Robyn prefers the green one from Bicheno the best. She asks for my opinion but doesn't really want it. I stammer an agreement to her. It's simply easier.

We're both reclining on the L-shaped divan in the living space. The curtains are drawn, although I can still hear the winds and torrential storm outside. The gas fire is on, as there's a chill.

I begin a conversation, trying hard not to say anything that will upset Robyn. 'I was…rea-reading something that might be of interest to you, my…my love.'

'Knowing you, that's extremely unlikely, but do go on, little Davey. Dazzle me with your sparkling knowledge. I'll try not to laugh.'

I pause, realising that she's not in the best of moods.

'Well…I'm waiting,' she prompts, more loudly.

'Okay. Do…do you kn-know where the word sou-sou-souvenir comes from?'

She folds her arms across her chest and glares at me with that impatient look that she uses so often.

I continue, having been granted her tacit agreement. 'Souvenir?' It's

Fr-French for to remember! I su-suppose that's why we call them souvenirs because they help us to…re-remember.'

That glare of hers is more intense now. 'Is that it? You really are full of useless information, you pathetic thing! What made you think I'd be interested in that rubbish? No…wait. You don't think, do you! You're only trying to annoy me, again. Great, useless slug!'

I turn away from her as she begins to move, yet I'm too slow and her knee catches me in the small of my back. As I wince in pain, she kicks again and I fall off the divan onto the thinly carpeted floor.

Later, she allows me to sit down again upon the divan. I make sure that I don't speak to her until she lets me know that she's forgiven me. It only takes her forty minutes, which is quite quick, considering.

After we watch her favourite television shows, she invites me to massage her thigh.

'If you make me feel good, then perhaps I'll let you do it.'

'You mean make love?'

She grunts. 'If it will shut you up for a month or so, I'm willing to let you, Davey. Even a dog deserves a treat now and then.'

I know that her idea of making love to me involves constantly asking me 'Have you finished yet?' while she noisily crunches on a packet of crisps.

She hitches her nightie to expose the naked flesh. I reach out tentatively only to cringe as she screams, 'No! You haven't washed those horrible handies, yet. I'm not letting you contaminate me with your icky germs. Go out and scrub them this instant!'

When I return, she examines them scrupulously, giving her approval with another grunt. I know she won't tolerate me doing anything else wrong.

Trembling a little, I begin to speak.

> 'Soft as satin, soft as silk,
> Smooth as creamy buttermilk.
> Caress your skin with oils and scent,
> I await your sweet consent.'

I recite her special words slowly.

She waves her arm grandly. 'You may proceed, my lowly slave.'

I pour her precious liquid onto my cupped hand to warm it then reverently my fingers brush her leg, gently rubbing her special oil onto her golden-tan skin. She sighs.

Is this why I allow myself to be humiliated? Love? No, it's not love. Lust then! I still don't understand why we have sex. She knows I enjoy it, so it's probably her tempting me with her power. If she gave me nothing, then maybe I would leave, denying her the means to pay for her extravagant lifestyle.

Usually I'm only allowed to watch her with her other men, although occasionally there's only the two of us. I'm hoping tonight will be special and that she'll start to love me again, treating me with respect from now on. I'm not optimistic.

She slaps my cheek; a hard, stinging slap. 'Naughty! That was too high. Just for that, you can sleep in the car tonight.' Her tone is angry, commanding. I've heard it before…too often.

She has pulled the duvet over her legs and waits expectantly as I dress. Her arms are folded. She's pouting. 'How dare you spoil our holiday, like that, Davey. I'm very disappointed in you, very disappointed indeed.'

I want to yell at her, to tell her she couldn't be as disappointed as me. I don't. Instead I open the door of the caravan. The rain is still lashing down.

'And leave the door unlocked. I'm expecting the waiter from the clubhouse. He should be here soon. It'll make a change to have a real man and not some stammering…'

At that moment, a car drives by, its high beam blinding me momentarily. I blink.

The light illuminates it all; Robyn's angry face, the caravan, the sodden mud path to the car and me, staring at my reflection in the rain streaked windows of the neighbouring van.

Is that really me? A nothing man with a nothing wife?

It's then I realise that my desire for her is no longer enough. I deserve better. Dave-rule. Number one.

*

'Excuse me…' Someone's speaking to me. I'm in the shop. The American is standing opposite.

'Sorry… Guess I was daydreaming. Sorry about that. Has Lynda sorted you out?'

'Oh, yes. We bought a few things. However, there's one other thing. I wonder if you sell bookmarks. Not those cardboard ones, though. Can you help at all? We always buy one when we visit somewhere new.'

'No problem! I know the sort you want. My wife's into bookmarks in a big way.' I point out the selection of leather ones at the end of the counter.

'Ah, a fellow collector. Is that your wife? She's an attractive young lady.' He nods towards Lynda, who is rearranging some shelves.

'Oh, no,' I laugh. 'My wife left me a while ago. We're separated and now…well, she travels a lot these days.'

Mr Tourist selects a pale green bookmark. He comments on the supple texture. It's emblazoned with the name of our town along with the harbour which is our claim to fame. Placing it in a bag, I watch the Americans move toward the shop door.

'By the way, which state are you from?' I call out.

'Kentucky. The Bluegrass State. Why do you ask?'

'Just curious,' I reply, as they walk out of the shop. It's interesting to know where my special gifts will travel to.

I move down the counter to tidy the souvenir selection. Postcards – looking sparse. I'll have to order some more on Friday. The furry animals grin inanely at me as I reposition them. Finally, there's the leather bookmarks. They've been a steady seller. Only fifteen left in the stand and eight of those are red. Lynda joins me and, since we have a few moments without customers, I kiss her deeply, affectionately…the way that lovers should kiss. She smiles back at me. She suggests some coffees and I ask her to get some more bookmarks from the store room while she's there.

While she's gone, I caress the tips of my fingers against the soft leather bookmark on top. This one is still its natural colour, a golden tan.

'Mm,' I begin softly, as I close my eyes to concentrate on the touch, the texture. My whisper is tinged with memories of the past. 'Soft as satin, soft as silk…'

Rainz

He noticed the change in the air first of all. There was a newly arrived subtle, dusty taint. It was not a smell that could be described in detail, more a whiff of clay talc in the gentle breeze, stirred and enhanced by moisture.

The sound would be next, or rather the absence of it. Countryside noise would be dulled and absorbed, like spilt ink soaking into well-used blotting paper on a desk. He smiled at the image. Times had changed from the pen nibs that scratched words across the pages of his schooldays. Only nature remained eternal – the sound and touch of a raindrop were the same now as they had always been.

The old man fidgeted in his attempt to get more comfortable, then gazed at the irregular blue horizon for the usual signs of coming rain. They were the same hills which heralded childhood storms a lifetime ago. He could not discern any warning today – only a grey haze at the land-sky boundary. Maybe that was it, he considered, frustrated at his failing eyesight.

The sun had long since departed, along with its cooling shadows. The colours of the native garden blooms were not as vibrant now but were still testament to the warmth of the summer's day. Slowly he turned at a nearby sound, half-expecting his daughter to be coming so she could take him inside. She was his youngest, a mother-to-be herself. She would come soon, caring for him now that he could no longer care for himself.

His attention was drawn to a flash of tinted movement, near the earlier noise. He turned his head, straining to focus on the cause of the momentary excitement that he felt. Although it might be nothing, he welcomed any stimulation to his day-to-day tedium. There it was: a male robin, constantly alert in its explorations. For a moment, it came near to him, realised its error and flew off again. For some reason, he felt sad and envious at the same time; sad since he would have loved to share the robin's adventures for a few more minutes, and envious because the small bird still was full of energy with its life still to live while he… No, that wasn't fair. He had experienced such happiness already and was determined to fight the problems that now assaulted him. It was only a stroke and although his body might be ravaged for the present, his mind wasn't, and his mind had always been his greatest strength.

The hush altered slightly as a single raindrop fell to a dried leaf on the parched earth. He peered intently to witness the change in dappled colour of the leaf from beige to burnt umber. The rain had proclaimed its coming to the parched landscape all around him. He wondered about his daughter. Surely she knew and would come to move him from the certain storm. She wouldn't leave him in the open. She wouldn't.

Another droplet splashed nearby. It also disturbed the tranquillity of the leaf litter. Where was she? Touching the wheels of his chair to push them, he knew instinctively that his strength had gone. He could not move himself to shelter. The exercises to help restore some movement to his partially paralysed body had only begun the previous week and he already could move his fingers again, even if it was only a little.

There was a gentle silent sigh in resignation at the possibility that he might get wet. The first rain in five months. He recalled another lazy, dry summer like this. It was long ago when he ran freely around these same gardens. At that time, he was filled with the energy and joy of a child. So many years gone. And yet, in some aspects, it was yesterday to him. His mother standing, arms crossed over the lilac-spotted apron she always wore. Her manner was gentle, always helpful, and he recalled her smile. In his thoughts, the old man heard himself once more. 'Rainz, Mama. Look at the rainz,'

A cooling splash licked the greying hairs of his bared arm. More spots followed, cast down from the leaden skies. He rejoiced in the movement, the activity, the sensations of his changing feelings.

There was one solitary droplet hanging precariously on a leaf close to his feeble sight. It was a thing of boyhood fascination – a shimmering rainbow. It beckoned him to reach out to touch it.

Gazing upwards, he closed his eyes against the increasing assault, all concerns forgotten about becoming wet. It was too late. Already his sodden clothing swathed his frail body. He thought again of his daughter. Why isn't she here? His worries were now for her, rather than himself.

The hard rain beat against his closed eyes. He felt life forces of nature tumbling about him, protecting and renewing his spirit-drained soul. 'Rainz,' he recalled in his exhilaration.

The precious waters transformed the dry garden and countryside, enhancing the colour of the plants wilted by the summer warmth. All around the glistening figure of the old man life was being renewed. Accepting his own fate as a part of the same life cycle, he smiled inwardly at the energy bestowed on him. An opened mouth allowed the waters to rejuvenate his inner self at the same instant that it bathed his sun-weathered skin.

Overhead, the thunder rumbled across the clouds, preceded by sudden flashes of strobed whiteness. He relaxed while sharing the loud declaration of nature's majesty.

The wheelchair moved. Instinctively he tensed. What was happening? He felt himself pushed to the shelter of the veranda as the storm continued. Grudgingly, he accepted the disturbance, aware that his time of union with the rain was now over.

His daughter moved around to face him. Her hair was dishevelled, her demeanour confused. She must have been sleeping. 'Why didn't you call me?' she demanded, both concerned and guilty.

His eyes replied.

Instantly, Julie regretted her accusations. 'Because you couldn't,' she understood from his plaintive appearance, sobbing at the reminded truth.

'It's all right,' his eyes continued through the tears. Slowly, he pulled himself upright and demanded for her to look at him. 'Rain,' he whispered. A single coherent word forced through the haze of his now-language.

The old man smiled, knowing she was sharing his pleasure at the brief respite from aridity for the fourth generation ancestral home. And he smiled because he knew he would learn to speak again. It was only one word but he knew it was the right word; the first proper word since his stroke. It might take some time, but he could do it…with the help of his loving family and the determination to be himself again.

Julie replied, realising at the same time that the father she thought that she'd lost was still there. 'Yes, Dad. That's right. Rain!'

A Crooked Little Smile

It's early November and it's raining. The type of never-stopping, saturating rain that deafens me as it pounds upon the veranda iron roof. The type of rain that makes me even more depressed than I am already.

Three golden leaves float by on the silver rivulet which used to be our path. They have served their summer purpose, only to be discarded when they began to wither in the cooler nights. Brown leaves…useless leaves.

Nevertheless, I suppose I can relate to them. I'm not much use myself at the moment. My usual vibrant personality is gone, my speech is almost impossible to understand now and my face…well, let's say that it's seen better days.

I've been off work for the past six weeks, trying to get myself better, trying to restore my life. So far, there had been no improvement in either. I'm suffering from a type of facial paralysis called Bell's palsy. One side of my face has died. They say it's temporary, while giving me tablets and electrical stimulation to fix the nerve. They say I'll be able to smile again and not scare small children. They tell me lots of things while usually avoiding eye contact, yet no one will tell me when I'll look normal once again.

In between visits to doctors and clinics, I've sat on my favourite bench here, on the veranda. It's the ideal place to feel sorry for myself since we don't have any nearby neighbours or close friends to attempt cheering me up. I can't go to work due to my new 'good' looks and I certainly don't want to see anyone. All in all, I'm quite content to sit here and watch the leaves dying as autumn turns to winter.

My cat's sharing the bench with me. She doesn't pass any

judgement. Even Mike, my husband, is staying away more often. He says he's busy at work and maybe he is. I know he's not around much these days. I remember the expression on his face the first time he saw my face. Concern, horror…whatever it was in his eyes, I doubt he'll ever look at me again without recalling that shock.

I felt different that first day because my eyes couldn't cope with the sunlight outside. Within hours, my left facial muscles had stopped working. Eyes, mouth all hanging loosely. Speech was slurred, I couldn't close my eyelid; it was a nightmare. My boss came out to home. I don't think he believed me until he saw me dribbling coffee out of my mouth. I couldn't face him after that. He agreed that I couldn't do my job if no one could understand what I was saying.

Thinking of coffee, it's about time to have one. The training baby mug helps avoid the spills though it doesn't do much for my self-confidence. I must do the speech exercises too. I need a mirror for that.

Damn door – it's blown shut. I'll have to walk around to the kitchen through silver rivers and soggy grass and…and now the bloody rain's getting heavier. Great! I'll be soaked. I swear using one of those words that mother says isn't very 'ladylike'. Even that comes out wrong. I pause for a moment, wondering. If someone swears but no one knows, is it really swearing? I swear again, louder and more carefully. It sounds better this time, definitely more satisfying.

I'd prefer not to get my hair wet. There's a bag on the seat. It's got the tape and scissors to help close my eyelid when I sleep, along with other stuff from the physio; pamphlets, booklets, telling me about the causes and paralysing effects of the infection. It's a shame none of the expensive colour literature tells you how to deal with the loss of confidence, or how to deal with children who stare and point, or adults who look away.

Lifting the bag, I empty the contents out then carefully cut two eye slits in the brown paper. Not very fashionable, but it'll keep my head dry.

There's a noise behind me. The door opens and Mike sticks his head out. 'Hi, sweets. I'm home.'

It's not even two o'clock. I try to ask why he's early. The words slur together. He's gone again and the door's ajar.

For the past four weeks, I've rarely seen him. That's probably a good thing from his point of view and I haven't pressured him about it. Wives with deformed faces aren't the greatest turn-on. I feel that I'm losing him. It's just that…I've needed him and he's not been there.

Looking down at my hands holding the bag, I know that I need him now. I begin to cry a little. I…need him to kiss me and hold me, to cuddle me, to love me.

When he comes out to the veranda again, I'm standing there naked, the paper bag placed neatly over my head. My head is lowered, probably at the humiliation of my actions. I watch another dead leaf drift by as droplets torment it from above. I turn my head slowly, watching it on its last journey and then my vision blurs with my own tears. Lord, I hate myself.

'Mike. Make love to me. I… I'll keep the bag on if it helps you,' I mumble as distinctly as I can. I'm able to hear the rain but there's no reply from him. I turn to peer through the slits at my husband and rub my eyes.

He's covering his mouth with his hands. He's laughing? At me? I feel so angry.

To his side, I can see my reflection in the front door. A woman's body with a brown paper head. Lord, is that me? No wonder he's laughing. What was I thinking? The original PBJ – paper bag job.

He comes to me, enfolding me, hugging me so close. I begin to giggle also as he removes the bag tenderly to kiss my crooked lips.

'What's going on in that crazy mind of yours? No…let me guess. You think I've gone off you because of your face. Is that it?'

Blushing, I nod. I feel the warmth and comfort of him cuddling me. 'You're always working late,' I try to say.

'I've been making changes for our surprise holiday. I've arranged to have the next three weeks off to spend with you.'

Three weeks. Mike virtually carries the business. Obviously he's got some of the others to pull their weight.

'Holiday? I don't want to go away. I don't want people to see me,' I protest.

'We're not going away. We'll sort this out together, at home. I'll be here to take you to the hospital each day and you can help me learn to cook. We'll get through this together.' He kisses me on my eyebrow, my nose, my cheek, my lips.

'You know what, my little lover?' he whispers in my ear as he nuzzles it. 'Your eyebrow moved. I could feel it. Guess you're on the mend. Now let's get inside where I can warm you up. Our holiday starts now.'

The Sound of Rain

Rain didn't come all that often to the Aussie outback, but when it arrived it was usually with a vengeance: storm force winds, driving sheets of unrelenting downpours and lightning that illuminated the night skies. Even the roos usually hopped for cover.

Today was one of those times.

'You sure you shut them doors to the barn, girlie?'

'Yes, Dad. And please don't call me girlie. I'm thirty-one years old.' I peered out the window to where the big, old shed should be. Even though it was only a hundred metres from us, all I could see was a shimmering grey curtain.

'Sorry, Courtney. I keep forgetting you're all grown-up. I keep forgetting lots of things…' His voice trailed off.

I was a farm girl, born and raised. But now, caring for Dad and trying to manage everything, I kept thinking more and more about what I was missing out on: a social life, my own career, marriage.

This wasn't what I'd wanted. I'd been doing okay in the Big Smoke, Canberra, with my consultancy business. Then it all went wrong. Mum passed away and my brother, Kyle, went to England with his wife to care for her mother. That left me to return home to help Dad cope. Goodbye dreams…at least for the foreseeable.

I didn't resent anyone. It was one of those things. Even though I loved farming, Kyle was always the strong one, meant to take over running things. Doing the heavy work was a struggle for me, even with Dad's help.

As for wet weather, I generally adored it. Whether we had a shower with its gentle pattering on our iron roof or an ordinary downpour, demanding attention, I loved the sound inside.

But today was a biblical deluge, far more destructive than any storm I'd seen before. No one could stand in those gales and sweeping torrents.

'I said, the phone's ringing, Courtney,' Dad shouted, obviously for the second time. The overhead din was deafening.

It never rang these days, apart from Kyle calling from Cheshire to check on us. I rushed to answer it, covering my other ear to listen.

'That you, sis? Car's stuck in a hole. I need your help.'

'What? To ring the AA or whatever they're called over there.'

'I'm not in Cheshire. I'm about four k down the track. That ford through Kookaburra Creek.'

I almost dropped the phone. Kyle was here?

'Supposed to be a surprise. Trust me to pick the one day we have the granddaddy of thunderstorms.'

The creek was usually a few dirty puddles but today it would be a raging torrent. If Kyle was in the middle, he needed help fast.

'I'll get the tractor,' I told him.

'The Steiger.' It was the largest one we had.

'What about Dad?'

'Bring him. He can drive it better than you.'

Kyle was right of course. It was a brute to handle and I'd been treating Dad as an invalid for so long, I'd forgotten what he was capable of.

I explained Kyle's predicament to Dad as we grabbed our wet weather gear. On impulse, I grabbed my arrows and bow. I'd need something to reach Kyle stuck out in the stream's centre. An arrow line seemed the best option.

Opening the farmhouse door, we were immediately lashed by the full force of the gale. I helped support Dad as we made a dash for the sheds.

We soon had the five-hundred-horsepower beast churning through the waterlogged track up towards the creek. I watched Dad in the swivel seat as he took control. It was crowded for me on his left yet I was impressed to see my father taking charge again. I often suspected that he'd given up on himself when Mum passed. Now, with Kyle in trouble, my childhood hero was back.

The rain sounds reminded me of the twofold nature of rain in the bush: part blessing, part destructiveness. Life out here was a balance. I'd seen what the sunshine did to the crops and the sheep in the drought years. Having fair skin and freckles, I'd had my share of sunburn as well. With the rainfall, I felt safe. Mum used to laugh about my 'rain bathing' as I stood in the summer storms.

I used to love how the longed-for rain assaulted my senses when it arrived; the cascade of dancing raindrops, the lovely smell in the air as the first drops fell. Mum told me that special, beautiful scent had a name – 'petrichor'.

The tractor jolted as it hit a boulder on the road. I stopped daydreaming; Dad was concentrating hard, the tractor now in high gear as it splashed through the waves of rainfall. He was worried. So was I.

Fortunately, the visibility was improving as we neared the creek.

'There he is, Dad,' I exclaimed, spotting Kyle's four by four in the midst of the chaotic maelstrom.

It was tipped to one corner. The gravel ford must have given way under the swirling eddies of mud and vegetation.

By now the dusking was descending yet Kyle flashed his lights. He was all right.

We ran to the water's edge. Unfortunately, his SUV shifted at that moment. Although the rain was lessening, the creek torrents weren't. The waters were almost up to the top of the wheel arches. I hoped that Kyle had had the presence of mind to attach a tow rope to the front jate rings before the water had risen much, otherwise recovery would be virtually impossible.

He'd wisely decided against swimming to safety, considering the trees and debris that were tumbling by him. There was even a tree bouncing against the side of the vehicle, seemingly caught under the chassis. He held a coiled tow rope out of the window, indicating it was attached. There was no way he could throw it to us on the bank or for anyone to wade or swim to get it.

Dad saw the solution before me. I was panicking yet he was thinking clearly.

'The log, gir– Sorry, Courtney.'

I nodded, soaking despite my Akubra and waterproof Duster, returning with my kit and compound bow. I was aiming for the wooden tree trunk caught on the car. Shooting an arrow into the vehicle wasn't an option despite Kyle often saying I was as good as Robin Hood.

'Steady, Courtney,' Dad said gently.

The arrow fell short. Kyle's vehicle shifted again, tilting over even more.

'One more time, Courtney. Make it count.'

I nocked the aluminium arrow once again, and took a deep breath before releasing the bowstring. This time, the arrow struck the tree just below the passenger window. Kyle reached out to grab the line then tied it to the tow rope.

Little by little, we teased the rope to the shore until Dad grabbed it firmly to attach to the Steiger. The torrential rains had returned and the night was closing in. Just as I could sense that Kyle would be okay, a movement from upstream caught my attention. Through the shadows I could see the white water and light bark of a ghost gum. The huge tree was being pushed over the rapids towards us and if it hit the SUV, it would turn it over, bashing it to shreds. My brother wouldn't stand a chance.

Dad saw it too and climbed quickly into the cab. The race between us and the tree was going to be close. I watched, hardly daring to breathe as the tow rope tightened and the big Tier engine took the strain. At first nothing happened.

I realised Dad knew what he was doing. Too quickly and the rope might snap and whip back at us.

With a jolt, the SUV climbed out of the hole onto the remaining level ford and was pulled slowly towards the bank. The gum crashed into the back of it causing the vehicle to turn yet it kept moving to safety until it broached the creek bank.

Kyle jumped out as I sloshed through the mud to embrace him. 'I knew I could count on you, little sis. And Dad too,' said Kyle.

Dad and I returned home in the Steiger with Kyle following.

Forty minutes later, we all sat down in the lounge. The casserole I'd prepared earlier was reheating and would easily be enough for three. I had a zillion questions to ask now we could talk to one another without shouting.

'Well, why are you here, Kyle? And why not tell us you were coming home?' I said, sipping a hot drink.

He smiled that knowing smile of his. Kyle always liked his secrets. 'Donna and I decided to come back here to the farm. We missed it and both of you so much. Besides, we wanted you to get back to that big exciting city life.'

Then he ruffled my already dishevelled hair. 'Let's face it, sis. You're not really cut out for life as a bushie. You love wearing that lippy and those posh frocks of yours, don't you? Can't see you shearing sheep wearing designer high heels.'

'But what happens to Donna's mum back in the UK? I thought she was still a bit crook.' Her illness was the reason they went there, after all. What Kyle was saying didn't make any sense. True, I did prefer the nightlife in the Big Smoke yet there was no way Donna could stay away from her mum for long.

'It was so simple when I thought about it. She comes to live with us over here. We have stacks of room and Donna's mum and our dad get on like a house on fire, don't you, Dad?'

I looked over to Dad who, like me, was trying to take it all in.

'Donna's coming with her mum? Sounds great. Better make the spare beds up, Courtney. And…'

'It's all right, Dad. He didn't mean now.' I saw him relax again.

Kyle continued. 'I came on ahead. It took a bit of doing but Donna's mum is emigrating and looking forward to her new life here.'

We chatted a bit more over dinner. It did sound perfect. The sprawling farm house was more than large enough for everyone.

As Dad cleared up, I wandered out onto the veranda with Kyle. The showers on the curved roof sounded comforting now, steady and refreshing. Stars were peeking out from the dissipating clouds.

'Dollar for your thought, little sis.'

'The rain. It always brings change. Flowers, green grass for the sheep, full rainwater tanks. I guess today's a change for me, too…for all of us.'

'I saw a different side to Dad today.'

'Yeah. So, did I. More confident and in control. I think having you all here will be great for him.'

'And what about you, Courtney? What are your plans?'

'That's it. Now I have choice. Maybe back to the city. Maybe set up my internet biz from here. No great rush. In the city, life can sometimes be so hectic that you forget to listen.'

'Listen? Listen to what?'

'People. Your own thoughts and desires.' I sat down on the big swing seat and patted the cushion by my side.

Kyle joined me.

'But right now, let's just sit here quietly and listen to the rain.'

One of Those Things

It's two twenty-three in the morning. I'm exhausted and I can't sleep and it's bucketing down outside. On my left, Rod's sleeping soundly; his heavy breathing is not helping my insomnia. How can men switch off so easily?

I gaze around the cramped space with its torn chintz curtains still visible in the light from the street lamps outside. It's not exactly the pinnacle of luxury. Still, it was all we could afford when Rod arrived a week ago. It was soon after the police told us about the accident.

He's done so much in that week, so I don't really begrudge him his rest now. He'll need all of his strength for the days ahead. We both will.

We were still in our nightclothes when the police rang the doorbell. We put our crumpled dressing gowns on and sat on the settee drinking tea from chipped mugs and considered all the matters that needed to be dealt with.

'Just one of those things,' the policewoman told us as we both sat on our settee in shock.

Rod checked the internet, found this…this cheap caravan to rent before he drove down to sort everything out.

I came by train yesterday. He collected me in our car and we'll return home tomorrow. The journey will take us most of the day; the first day of our new life together.

I'm not sure if I can do it, though. And that's the main reason that I can't sleep. I mean, how the hell do you become an instant mother overnight with hardly any warning?

Rob's ex had died in a traffic accident. Her name is…was Jennifer. We didn't ask if she'd been driving while drunk again or if it was someone else's fault. It didn't matter. She was dead. Rob sat there quietly while I clasped his hand. He'd loved her once and had told me about the good times they'd shared.

They'd had a baby girl, Mandy, and then she'd left him to go off with a footballer she'd met at the club where she worked. She'd taken Mandy with her. That was the last time that Rob had seen his daughter…that is, until last Sunday when he drove down here from home to see her in the hospital.

He phoned me on his mobile from there. I had never heard him cry before.

'They say she'll be all right, honey. She was unconscious when the paramedics brought her in. That's why the specialists weren't sure. But she woke up. Apart from her broken arm and the cuts and bruises, she's all right. At least Jennifer had enough sense to secure her properly in her car seat. It's all that saved her, apparently.'

The line went quiet for a few seconds as Rob struggled to compose himself.

I prompted him gently. 'Had Jennifer…you know?'

'Yeah…well over the limit. I just can't understand how she could think of driving…especially with Mandy in the car too.'

'And…and what about little Mandy? How is she…coping?' I asked, changing the subject. After all, Jennifer was gone. Mandy was our priority now. Jennifer had denied Rob any access to her. She never even sent Rob a photo or video. So much for paternal rights! The court believed all the lies she told them…her and her hotshot lawyer. Rob didn't have a chance. In any case, he wasn't in any fit state to oppose her back them. When she'd left him three years ago, he'd been a nervous wreck and she'd taken advantage of that to make sure he'd never see Mandy again.

'She's managing really well, sweetheart. All things considered. I'll send you a photo on my phone. Of course, she's injured but her golden hair… You should see it. It's long and wavy just like yours…and she has a little dimple on her cheek and gorgeous blue eyes. You'll…you'll love her, Shanna.'

'I'm sure I will,' I answered, trying to sound as positive as I could. We continued to talk for a while until I excused myself, telling him that I had something cooking on the stove that needed attention. After I put the phone down, I rang my mother. I needed someone to talk to…someone who would understand my apprehensions…someone who wasn't Rob.

Mum listened to me talking non-stop for almost ten minutes. Of course she already knew that Rob and I couldn't have children of our own. 'You tried so many times with IVF, Shanna. Now, because of this awful tragedy, you have an opportunity to be a mother yourself – a much-needed one.'

'I realise that, Mum. To be truthful, we reached the point where we accepted that we'll only have one another…and that was enough. We put all our energies into our careers and we were doing great…better than great. My promotion…I've worked so hard for it.'

'It's a matter of priorities, sweetheart. That little girl needs her dad now, but she'll need you just as much.'

She was right of course. She's always been more pragmatic than I am. And so I spent the rest of the evening deep in thought. Rob and I still loved one another deeply. However, with the death of Jennifer, Rob is the only relative that little Mandy has left; a father of whom she has no memory.

Rob has always wanted access to his little girl and has missed being a part of her life. Now he has the opportunity to bring her into our home and become a proper father. I couldn't say no to him. She's his child. The problem for me is that she isn't ours and I'm so guilty for feeling that way.

The following evening, I tried to talk to Rob about my misgivings but naturally I held back expressing my innermost state of mind.

Nevertheless, a selfish part of me knew that our lives would have to change. From being a young career woman, I was afraid that I'd have to relinquish my fledgling career in management to become a full-time mum to someone else's toddler. I'm not sure that I can do that as willingly as Rob may want. After all, I love my work and we're both just starting to earn decent money. We planned on simple things to do with the extra…a better car, a new bathroom, maybe even a holiday overseas for a change. I don't think that Rob has considered that those plans may not happen now. He's spent the week clearing Jennifer's flat, arranging the funeral and making arrangements through social services for little Mandy. In between all that, he's been getting to know his daughter.

Oh lord. I just realised. Mandy probably wouldn't even know about him. She's all alone with strangers in that hospital, hurt, frightened, and then some strange man arrives. He tells her that he's her daddy and that she's coming to live with him now.

'Where's my mummy?' she must have asked at some time only to be told a gentler version of the sad truth: 'Your mummy had to go away.'

I feel so ashamed of myself. I never considered her at all; the torment she must be experiencing.

Taking care not to disturb Rob, I reach over to the broken melamine bedside table next to the bed and grope for my mobile. After it's firmly in my hand, I bring it near to my face but at the side of the bed so that the light doesn't wake him. I take a look at the photo that Rob sent me. The eerie light illuminates my side of the tiny bedroom and the rain drenched window.

She looks so sweet and vulnerable. Can I love her as my own? I'm still unsure, yet somehow, I feel more positive about the changes to our future lives. Even the rain sounds less irritating. Following one final long look at Mandy's image, I close my phone. Suddenly I feel quite sleepy and we have a big day tomorrow, don't we, Rob? As I snuggle up to his warm body, my eyes close. Yes, it's going to be a big day…

*

Later that morning, Rob is holding my hand as we sit in the hospital waiting room.

'The doctors have given her the all clear to come home today,' he explains to me. 'Trouble is, it'll be a different home with strangers living there. Us!'

'You've got all her toys and clothes. They'll help her to feel more comfortable…having familiar things with her. I know it's not the same as her mum but we'll be there for her…both of us.'

Rob takes a pink, fluffy puppy out of a carrier bag. 'This is her favourite, apparently. She told me that he was missing. He's called Spottie. Took me ages to find him. He'd fallen through a hole in the floor in that dump Jennifer was renting. I've washed him, ready for Mandy.'

I hold the fluffy dog in my hands. If he's important to Mandy, he's important to us.

Rob continues as he looks anxiously through the glass panelled door to the corridor. They said it would be better to meet in this family room. The name makes me feel warm inside.

'There wasn't much else of Mandy's to bring. I'm afraid Jenny's priorities were to buy more alcohol…not toys or pretty clothing for her little girl.'

'Well, that's one thing she won't be short of with us. I've already bought her some new dresses. I just hope they'll fit.'

'I'm sure they will, kitten. And thanks…for what you're doing. I do understand what I'm asking of you but we'll make it work…together.'

I haven't seen her yet. The nurses are dressing her in one of the new dresses I've brought along. Then they'll bring her to us. The paperwork and talks with social workers have all finished for the moment. Once we get home, other staff will come to visit us and we already have appointments with Outpatients at our local hospital for Mandy's follow-ups and physio.

As for me, I'm feeling so much better than I was during the night. The phone call from Mum first thing helped so much. She'd been busy ringing around to Rob's family as well as ours. Dad and Mum have assured me that I'll be able to continue full-time work if I want.

I've already arranged to have this week off, since Rob has to return to his job, Actually, I was ready to resign so that I'd be there for Mandy. Maybe I still might. However, now I can take my time deciding. Mum and Dad will do most of the day-to-day care for Mandy. They're both retired and Mum confessed quietly that she was really looking forward to being useful again. She also admitted, with a laugh, that having someone else around apart from Dad would save her sanity. They both needed a new purpose in their lives and couldn't imagine anything more wonderful than helping to care for their new little grand-daughter.

Mandy should be here any moment. As for me, my stomach feels as though it's crammed full of butterflies with a bunch of moths joining in. The door's opening. I can hear her little voice outside. I wonder what she's thinking.

A nurse comes in leading Mandy with her good hand. She's looking around and when she sees Rob her little eyes light up. They've obviously bonded well.

He told me that three-year-olds are usually quite adaptable and unfortunately Mandy'll need to be. Everything she knew in her short life is being turned upside down. I wave to her.

She's much prettier than the photo. The injuries to her face are fading and her cheeky smile helps too. She doesn't appear too bothered with her broken left arm. I assume she's right-handed and realise there's a great deal that I don't know about her. It will be wonderful to find out and to teach her. Rob says she's bright and inquisitive but he would say that; he's her father.

She notices me and looks up at my eyes. After a moment, she asks hesitantly in a quiet voice, 'Hello. Are you my new mummy?'

I wasn't prepared for such a direct question this quickly; still, I smile and crouch down so that we're face to face. 'I... I guess I am, Mandy. Would you like to give me a mummy-hug?'

I open my arms as she walks forward, slowly at first. I notice her glancing at Rob to assess his reaction. If it's all right with him, then she will do it. He crouches down too and nods. I enfold her gingerly, conscious of her arm in its plaster cast and sling.

'My little daughter.' Yes, I decide. Mandy and I are going to get on wonderfully.

Storm

Snuggled between gentle green hills, the village fell into darkness as the clouds tumbled toward it. Gusts buffeted the crops causing Agapios to stare upward and make his decision. Storms were unusual for this time of the seasons. Nevertheless, precautions were still required. Directions were given to concerned mothers who went forth to shepherd their children inside the flimsy houses. Animals were gathered too as mighty winds heralded the coming rains amidst the Stygian skies.

Agapios glared at Thanos. 'Fine and sunny with a chance of afternoon sprinkles?'

'What can I say? I just read the goat's intestines. I don't make the weather.'

'Unless you get your act together, it won't be goat's intestines we'll be using, Thanos. But right now, we have to get everyone under shelter.'

The women tried their best to calm the little ones, though they themselves shook with fear at the sound of distant thunders. Only one mother was without her son. She knew where he was, and that he would not return to the township. For that, Alcmene was angry at him, at his father, as well as herself for her own past stupidity. Still, she could not change him nor did she want to. Her son had his own great destiny to fulfil.

Away from the others, the athletic youth surveyed the storm front. The hairs on his head stood to a limp attention, and then danced slowly in the charged atmosphere. It was dark under the cumulus clouds that now glowed periodically as short flashes hopped across the heavens. He smiled, turning his face upwards to the rainstorm. Next, thunder rumbled in warning as he prepared himself.

'Anytime you're ready!' he shouted, hands cupped around his boyish face.

As if in answer, the skies flashed with golden sparks of such might that the very earth quivered in sympathy. A jagged crack split the heaven, arcing through the ionised air from clouds to the ground. It struck scant metres from the youth. He danced to one side, narrowly avoiding a second bolt which scorched the grasses beneath his feet.

Still he grinned, alive with the same energy gathered in the air around him. He kept his gaze skyward, anticipating the next assault, watching the thunderheads as the ozone permeated his surroundings. 'Missed!' he screamed into the rains.

Three strikes descended in response to his bravado. The brash youth nimbly avoided their fury.

The atmosphere was alive with lines branching like giant radiant cracks across a glassine sky. Once they had shattered the darkness with flashes of heaven-scented whiteness, they vanished instantly to leave no trace of their existence.

None of these bolts came close enough to hurt the boy as he leapt across the charred grasslands. The staccato lighting strikes continued crashing around him before they became fewer and fewer and stopped.

He seemed disappointed. 'I'll give you one last chance, old man. Give me all you've got.'

As if in answer, a phalanx of superbolts descended, aimed directly at the teenager. They shattered the rocks where he had been and rendered asunder the very ground so that only a jagged chasm remained. In spite of that, the youth stood atop a hill, having bounded to safety at the last instant, his eyes shielded from the immense brightness.

At last, sunlight parted the clouds. The terrifying storm was done and the boy-child had won.

'Thank you. Can we play again next week?' the teenager shouted loudly to the dissipating thunderheads.

Zeus peered down from Mount Olympus to the hills of Sparta. 'Kids,' he thought, feeling so proud of his Earth-born son, Heracles.

The Girl in the Evening Rain

I peer into the dark recesses of the shop entrance. There are noises and I wonder if she may be there. It's unlikely but when you're obsessed with finding someone, you'll try everything.

Bored eyes gaze back at me. A woman's eyes, the only part I can see of her in the night shadows. She has a man with her. I can hear his primaeval grunts and barely discern the blacker outline of his body against the darkness.

She says nothing. Her eyes continue their impassive stare. If I could see her open mouth and the trickle of blood from it, I would realise the horrific truth. Instead, I mentally excuse myself and trudge on.

I must have made some noise, loud enough to be heard above the rain, because the man turns to face me. I notice his expression in the dull amber of the street lamps. He looks angry.

The scenes that I've witnessed on these storm-soaked evenings often filled me with revulsion. Muggers, addicts, prostitutes all haunting the shadows of doorways while the ordinary people were snug inside their own warm rooms.

In some ways, I identify with the street dwellers. I'm a part of their world and they a part of mine. We exchange greetings at times, familiar figures who pass one another with heads bent low against the downpours; a single word, more often a shrug.

It's teeming with rain, exactly like that night I met her years before. The downpour pounds incessantly upon my hat, making its angry wet sounds. Even the wide brim, turned down around my head, doesn't help. It may make me feel dryer, although, in reality, I'm soaked through. Looking down at a stained, discarded tissue lying in the gutter, I know exactly how it feels. I've only been walking twenty minutes.

Why were nights like this my only chance of finding her? Stupid question, asked in frustration. The answer is simple. On any other night she, and the others, would be wandering free, cavorting in the cool, evening airs.

It's only on these hell-shrouded nights that I have any chance of seeing her again, as she hides in the shadows and faintly lit doorways of the city. I survey the street. She could be anywhere.

Tall lamps struggle to illuminate the scene, reflecting from the raindrops and puddles alike. Even though the people and the dogs and prams are gone, the street appears more alive than ever. There are lines of light that sparkle through the rains, while splashing mirrors on the ground perform for my eyes alone with their constantly changing tableaux. And the sounds: regular, hypnotic…so soothing that you can relax into their embrace forever. It's beautiful. Simply beautiful. If only it wasn't so bloody cold and wet.

Is she here? Head bent low against the windy onslaught, I struggle along the footpath, pulling the coat collar tighter. In my pocket I feel for the single tangible reminder of her. It's there still, confirming the reality of our only meeting years earlier. I swear as some frigid water runs down my neck. Stopping in the middle of the street, I face skyward into the torrent.

'Where are you?'

Then I hear footsteps behind me, sloshing through the puddles; probably the man I've seen earlier. The woman with the staring eyes will be more likely sheltering within the doorway waiting for the next client.

I found Bath Kol sitting in a darkened doorway twelve years before. Initially I stood next to her, shivering, waiting for a pause in the downpour. I only had a suit on and it was no protection from the weather at all.

Hugging my arms around my body, I hopped from one foot to another in an attempt to keep warm. I knew she was there on the other side of the alcove between the display windows. She waited, calm, quiet, motionless; a silhouette in grey-black shadows. I was certain she was a woman from her long hair. As she sat patiently, she gazed blankly at the storm. She didn't acknowledge me.

After five minutes, the summer shower was worse. I felt uncomfortable, the same feeling you have in an elevator with strangers invading your personal space. I had to say something to at least let her know I wasn't being totally ignorant. She appeared to be pretty; thirty-something with a long dress wrapped tightly around her. The street lamps didn't show any more of her.

She noticed my head turn and half turned herself. I usually don't find it difficult to speak to people. Women, especially ones I like, can be a problem. Why was I feeling apprehensive, now? I didn't even know her.

'Shocking weather!' I blurted out. Instantly I felt like a fool.

She ignored me, continuing her longing gaze at the street. I grew angry. She could at least say, 'Yes, awful!' or 'No, I reckon it's lovely!'

She turned to look at my feet, her head bowed. Well, something prompted a response, although I couldn't understand what.

Her voice was soft, barely audible above the rains. 'I didn't realise you were speaking to me. Most men don't notice me, let alone want to talk.'

I was surprised. From what I could see, every man would have noticed her. She had a presence, even sitting in the dark.

'Of course I can see you. I was simply trying to be civil, that's all,' I said. 'Just forget I spoke, okay?'

I poked my head out into the rain, searching for another refuge. A street vendor was in his open van almost ten metres away. He was selling drinks and snacks but there was no one around to use his services. The storm seemed to have settled in.

She spoke again. 'Sorry. I didn't mean to offend you. I was

surprised that you'd talk to me. In any case, I wasn't being rude. If you notice me, you must be very gifted.'

I mellowed. Me? Gifted? Possibly my boss should listen to her. 'What's your name?' I asked in a gentler tone.

She laughed. I thought it strange since the question was quite ordinary.

'It's been so long since I was asked that. I rarely meet someone new. It's funny, that's all. My name, it's Bath Kol. Try to remember it, look it up when you return to your home. Then you'll realise that this night is special…for both of us.'

Okay, I thought. Simple question, complex answer. 'Look, Bath Kol. You…you don't know me so it won't bother me if you say no, but I'm cold and I'm hungry and I'm going to get food from that van out there. Can I offer you something too? No strings.'

She accepted and I dashed across, then returned clutching two soups and sandwiches. I held one of each out to her and sat down beside her. There was a sound from behind her.

Bath Kol saw me turn. 'It's okay. Thanks…for the food.'

We sat talking for a while. The rain stayed constant but I wasn't in a hurry to leave. No one was waiting for me at my home. It was strange. I felt an affinity between us although I was puzzled, drawn to her and wondering who she was at the same time. There were none of the indications that she lived roughly, no possessions that I could see apart from the dress. It was clean and intact. At least, all I could see in the dim lights. And she was pretty, beautiful even. She avoided eye contact with me, a fact I put down to shyness. I was wrong.

I asked her where she would spend the night, thinking to offer a dry place at my home if she'd nowhere else to go.

She laughed again. 'I'll be fine here, David. I usually spend the wet nights in the shelter of doorways. I hate the rain at night. It makes… well, let's say that it makes it awkward to get around. No offence but you're the first man in a long time who's…' She paused, taking hold of my hand.

'Who's what?' I inquired.

'Shown any interest in me. It's…it's a good feeling.' She tilted her head to one side as if concentrating. 'As for your thoughts, please don't hope that we'll meet again. We can't. We won't.'

'My thoughts? Sure, I like you but that's it. After all, we've only met a few minutes ago and we know nothing about each other,' I told her, lying through my chattering teeth. For some reason, I knew I was intrigued by this stranger.

She faced me and I saw Bath Kol's eyes for the first time. The irises were bright yellow. They had their own subtle glow and I knew at once the colour was not a trick of the street lamps.

'I'm sorry. Your words don't match your feelings. I never intended for you to feel any affection for me.'

'And what about you?' I asked. 'Do you have feelings for me at all?'

'If I did, it wouldn't matter. There are rules… Sorry, that's the wrong word. English is a complex language even for me. Not rules… precedents. I can't see you again, David Purkiss.'

It was at that moment that I realised that I'd never told her my name, even though she knew it. Other things that she'd said now began to make sense. It seemed impossible but nevertheless there was only one explanation.

'You can read my thoughts, can't you?'

Bath Kol nodded. 'Some. I try not to intrude.'

We sat in silence after that. Our hands were still clasped together. After five minutes, we both noticed the change of night sounds at the same time. The rain was stopping. We could go now, if we wanted. In retrospect, I could have left anytime. Okay, I might have got wet, yet I would have survived. Nowadays, I often think that it might have been better if I'd never stopped there in that darkened sanctuary. However, I did and we can't undo the past, can we?

When I wandered out onto the street to survey the clearing skies, I understood that I'd met someone that I could love.

'Bath Kol?' I called out.

There was no answer. I peered into the doorway only to discover she'd gone. Frantically, I examined the area all around, hoping to see her. Perhaps I should have looked more thoroughly. I would have if I'd realised at the time who Bath Kol was. Was there a note or some message? She wouldn't leave without a goodbye, would she?

As I made my way back to our doorway, I felt betrayed and sickened. There was nothing except the crumpled cups and papers of our meal together. No note, no sign she'd even been there.

I peered up and down the deserted street once more, a final time before leaving. There was something bright on the ground near the door front. It was only a feather. A single pure white feather.

On the next stormy night, I went back to that street. I walked for hours searching for her. Possibly she'd be huddled in a doorway on some other rain-soaked street. She wasn't there. Occasionally I'd go out again, although only when it rained, a diversion in my mundane life.

Now, twelve years later, it's an obsession that consumes me. On fine nights, I search books and newspapers, hoping to find a clue where she might be. When it rains, I roam the streets, with that feather clutched tightly in my hand.

It's still white, still perfect and, to add to its mystery, it's indestructible. Diamond-coated saws don't scratch it, furnaces leave it cool and inviolate, and the strongest acids turn to water. As I said, totally indestructible. No one else can see it, not unless I'm touching it. Then, well then, their minds won't accept it anyway and they return to their uncomplicated lives, their predictable lives, to their own little hiding places.

I've had ample opportunity to consider the events of that first night, to ponder on them, to ask others. I had a list of questions that I have to ask her: why me, was it chance or part of some plan that brought us together, and why did she leave me like that? Was it to dissuade me from pursuing her? If it was, then it failed. Was it because there could never be any more between us? I can't believe that either.

Or was it because she loved me too, on a far deeper level than she should have?

'You talking to me?' He's about my height and build. I've never been a violent person but I can be quite assertive when I need to be. He's holding a knife, though, and I can see it's already stained with blood.

He notices my glance at his hand and grins. 'You saw my face, Fancy Man. I can't have no witnesses.'

Witnesses? To what? Oh hell! The girl with the blank stare!

He lunges forward, quicker than I expected. The knife plunges into my right shoulder. I scream in pain. I pull away as he lifts the blade a second time, realising that I'm already too dazed to protect myself.

'No!' A female voice shouts from above.

Although the next moments are a blur, I sense someone between me and the madman, huge feathers shielding my blood-soaked body. She faces him as he stabs at her, cutting through both flesh and bone. In her pain, she lashes out. A mighty wing smashes against him and his body crunches against a wall. He lies still, hopefully dead. My rescuer turns to me, her wings gradually folding against her shoulders.

I look up to her. 'My guardian angel,' I say, gritting my teeth against the cold and the pain.

'Don't be ridiculous, David. I simply happened to be nearby.'

I see that one wing is damaged and that she has been stabbed as well. She holds her hand over a wound on her side.

'Now who's lying?' I ask her.

She grimaces. 'Is this what you call pain?'

For the first time that night, I can examine my Bath Kol. She's not the same as I recall. The murderer has seen her and wounded her. Her feathers are dull, even missing in places. The twinkle's gone from her eyes. She kneels down on the street, slumping forward from her obvious injuries. It doesn't make sense.

'Help is coming,' she gasps.

'I thought you were indestructible. That feather of yours…'

'I've changed. Love does that to you.' She gazes up at me.

At that point, we hear a loud cry from behind Bath. The angel falls forward, a knife in her back.

'Bitch!' he screams. 'Stinking, filthy bitch! That'll learn you.' He pauses, realising for the first time she had wings. 'What the…? Y-you're a freak.' He pulls the knife from her body, slashing her wings.

She remains motionless, face down on the wet pavement. I look for some help, but we're alone. Totally alone.

'Stop. She's a seraphim…an angel! You can't kill an angel!'

'Course I can. I already done two blokes and four girlies. An angel, eh? Nice looker. Maybe I'll take me time with her first.'

I have to stop him from killing her, yet I have no weapon. Frantically, I feel my pockets. Nothing except my wallet, house keys and the feather from twelve years before. The feather? It can cut through anything if it's held correctly.

'Hey. Why don't you kill me first, you bastard?'

He hesitates.

'Or are you scared of me?' I continue. I have to get him to come to me.

'Right. You talked me into it. You first, nice and quick. Then her.'

I clutch the feather tightly as he approaches, and pretend to cower, curling up into a foetal crouch. 'No…no. Please. I've changed my mind. You can kill her…just let me live.'

He laughs, despite the damage to his leg when Bath had tossed him into the wall. Then he reaches down to grab me by my muddy coat. I try to stand, to get away. He relaxes his guard for an instant, allowing me to reach him with my good arm.

'Go to hell!' I spit at him while thrusting the feather's barb into his chest. I hear and sense it cleave through his skin and muscle to reach is heart.

His eyes open wide as he tries to pull away. Too late. He falls on top of my prostrate body, thrusting the feather deeper into his convulsing body. Finally, I hear his last breath. I close my eyes at last, weak from the effort of killing this man, although more out of fear for the angel. I'm certain that she's dead also.

There's a hand shaking me. My shoulder hurts as though it's on fire.

'He's alive!' a female voice calls out.

Opening my eyes, I look around. Bath Kol said help was coming. The minister kneeling over me is soaking from the downpour. There are others. Priests, a rabbi, two nuns and what seems to be a Muslim cleric.

The minister sees my expression. 'The angel called to us. We all look out for the Divine Ones, whenever they need our assistance.'

I can see their concern for my angel. She's conscious but her wings are damaged beyond repair. Police and an ambulance come, more members of this special group. The cops talk to the various clergy while the paramedics treat Bath Kol and then me.

My shoulder is dressed, the bleeding stopped. The rain gives the whole scene a surreal appearance.

'How is she?'

'Her wings and immortality are gone but she'll be okay. I hope you were worth it.'

'What do you mean, worth it? I love her.'

'And she loves you. Love, compassion…it's changed her. She's not an angel any more. She's mortal now. She's human.'

I take a moment to digest that.

'She put her own existence in danger in order to protect you. We call it self-sacrifice. The angelic ones call it humanity.'

They move us to the waiting ambulance, where we at last can hold hands. Her yellow eyes are blue now, her hair is matted with dirt and blood. She's still so very beautiful.

'Long time no see,' I half-joke.

'It's all right. We've got all the time in the world now, my love,' she replies with a smile.

The Park

Kaleidoscope

They came during the first week of February when the summer sun was at its most intense. Butterflies. Thousands of butterflies. At that point, they descended upon the forests and fields surrounding the small town of Whitestone, covering the eight square k area in a rainbow cavalcade.

I went there to witness the phenomenon first-hand, although I had another reason to visit. I dearly wanted to see her again. Danielle and I had been the closest of friends through school yet we had grown further and further apart as our studies and interests took us in diverse pathways. Despite the years since we'd spoken, I was still in love with her.

Sadly, although she'd loved me too, she'd spent more and more of her time pursuing her career and fixation on her precious sciences. Now she was a successful well-respected ecologist whereas I…well, I enjoyed my teaching and writing the occasional poem. I knew that I'd never have the ambition that she had.

She was in Whitestone to study the butterflies along with her team of like-minded scientists from the university. I'd seen her being interviewed on television. She was still gorgeous. It was the day after the kaleidoscope began.

A group of butterflies has a few collective names of which 'a kaleidoscope' is one and 'a rabble' is another. The kaleidoscope sounded better to me because of the vibrant poetic image, I guess. I'd been searching for Danielle among the sparse trees when I saw one of her team clad in the same distinctive uniform that she had worn on television.

'G'day,' I said to the young woman. 'I'm looking for Danielle Thorp.'

'The prof? Sure. She's over there, by the blue trailer.' She pointed down a pathway through the undergrowth that was alive with the mélange of flying colours.

Alongside me walked people of all shapes and sizes, determined to experience a little of this enchanted wonderland. It was frantic, mystical and so beautiful; the intoxicating scent of flowers, tiny wings darting by me and the soft hum as insects flitted around. It seemed to me that every one of the more than four hundred species of butterflies in Australia was there. I even noticed the huge Priam's birdwing that was over eighteen centimetres in width. They had never been seen this far south in Australia.

Soon I saw Danielle busying herself with an array of gadgets and apparatus outside a van. She hadn't changed very much in the time since we had last seen one another. Her burnished copper hair was tied in a ponytail that swished over her shoulders as she examined the readouts.

'Danielle?' I called out as I approached. As she turned, it was clear that she didn't recognise me at first. It was the beard, I suppose.

'Adrian? Hey, I like the new look. It suits you.' She smiled and wrapped her arms around me before giving me a kiss on the creek.

The touch of her lips and fragrance of her favourite perfume brought back so many memories. If only she weren't so intense about her work.

She continued as she stood back from me, holding my hands in hers. 'I didn't expect to see you here. How are you?'

'Fine. A little on the tubby side but you…you look as pretty as ever.' I said. I noticed her looking upward at the multicoloured skies through her dark rimmed glasses. 'Actually, I knew you'd be here. The numbers are so amazing. Any idea what's happening?'

'If you want a scientific explanation, I can't give you one. We've been monitoring atmospherics, weather, solar activity, geographics… even lunar changes and chemicals from the plants themselves. It makes no sense. There's nothing special about this locality that might explain why there are so many butterflies.'

'Maybe there isn't a rational explanation, Danni. Have you ever considered that?'

'Rubbish! There's always a scientific explanation. Things like this don't just happen.' Lowering her voice, Danielle continued. 'Look, Adrian. I'm busy. I'm surprised you even want to talk to me considering what I said to you the last time we met. I've not changed and I doubt that you have either. Whatever we had wasn't enough for me. I believe in what I'm doing here. I have my work. I don't need distractions any more.'

She turned back to her readouts and monitoring equipment, dismissing me once again, yet I wasn't going to walk away as easily this time. The thought of those years of being without her by my side because I was a distraction in her eyes… It was time to make my stand. And if she still refused to see what we could have after today? Well. I couldn't think about that possibility. I could only think that there was a chance for us to be together again.

I swallowed whatever pride I had left and demanded she face me, even if my loud tone startled her. 'Danni, I came here for you and I believe that, deep down under that barrier you've built up around your emotions, you love me too, despite all your denials.'

Her eyes flashed with anger. I'd never seen her fuming in all the years we'd known one another. Even when she'd discovered the truth about her father, she'd never lost her temper, simply immersed herself in her studies and shut herself off from reality. It was the finish of our changing relationship as teenagers, as we were beginning to move from friendship to something much closer.

'How dare you! How can you possibly presume to know the way I think?'

'Then tell me truthfully. Do you really have no feelings for me?'

She paused, forcing herself to control her emotions. It seemed she was at least considering her answer and not simply dismissing me. Her expression softened. 'I…I do feel something for you, Adrian. It's as though I like you and hate you at the same time. It's tearing me up inside, so it's easier if you go away. At least then I don't have to decide.'

I reached across to hold her hand in mine. She let me, possibly shocked at her earlier outburst. I could see her eyes beginning to mist over.

'Danni. I'm not your dad. And you…you're not your mum.' I spoke quietly, not wanting to tear her apart more than I had already.

In her pale green eyes, I could see the hurt that was still there, the betrayal when her father left them for another woman. Following that, her mother's fury towards men in general must have caused her such conflict: wanting to be with me while being told that men were not to be trusted. No wonder she chose another way out, devoting herself to her studies instead.

She stared at me. The teenager whose smiling face had lit up my life was still there struggling to make sense of her mixed-up world. 'My dad. He hurt me so much.'

'I know. But I'm Adrian. I…am…not…your dad,' I repeated. 'I would never hurt you like he did.'

It was then that we were distracted as a shower of butterflies descended on the clearing. It was breathtaking. Despite the intensity of our discussion, I had to change the subject. I gestured all around us. 'Look around you at this…this miracle. Take a few minutes to see it for what it is…to appreciate the beauty and the joy that all of these other people are here to witness. Come with me for a walk…please.'

She stared back at me, arms crossed across her lab coat. Her body language said it all. She wasn't going to come. Despite my love for her, I wasn't going to beg her. I still had some pride.

At that moment, a young bloke ran up to Danni. He was quite excited and was holding a specialised capture jar in his hand. I don't think he realised I was there and that he was interrupting us.

'Excuse me. I've found this specimen, professor. I can't identify it, so it must be rare.'

Instantly she returned to that impersonal persona that she used to shield herself from her emotions. 'Let's see what you have, Paul. And Adrian, if you've got a moment, I'd appreciate your ideas. You were always the expert on the unusual ones.'

Danni and I stared at the imprisoned butterfly, at its unique blue and white markings on gossamer wings. We both recognised it instantly, although it had been seventeen years since we had studied photographs of this particular species.

'It's a female Xerces blue!' we declared simultaneously.

Danielle turned to me. Her voice was quivering. 'But that's simply impossible. It's…it's extinct. Nineteen forty-one, I think.'

'And it was only native to California. What is it doing here?'

Although I wasn't an expert entomologist like Danielle, we had both been avid amateurs in studying butterflies while we wandered through the wildflower meadows near our homes. Danni had made a profession of it, whereas I had only continued to do so as a hobby. In some ways, that was a testament to Danielle's enthusiasm on the subject, although I also realised that it made me feel closer to her and the fantastic times we once shared.

Over the ensuing hour, Danielle continued studying the live specimen while she and I talked properly for the first time in years. I could sense that she was finding this conundrum difficult to cope with. All her life she had been convinced that science always had the answers.

Danni was always great at multitasking, so she could laugh as we reminisced at the same time as she engaged in taking precise measurements. Irrespectively, she was thorough in her studies. Once she'd finished her deliberations, she told me what I'd suspected all along.

'No doubt about it. It's *Glaucopsyche xerces*, Adrian – the Xerces blue. I thought it might have been its cousin, the silvery blue, but it isn't. Here we have a butterfly that has been listed as extinct for over seventy years.' Her joy was electric yet it was tempered with a myriad of questions that she couldn't answer.

'What are you going to do with it, Danni?' I asked her. 'You can't honestly want to keep it in a jar for the rest of its short life?'

She pondered that question for a few seconds. 'It's my job as a scientist. It's the only way to prove we've seen this beautiful creature. We have it fully documented of course…photos, video; but to actually have a live specimen to study further?'

'If you release it, there's a chance it will mate and the species will continue. Sometimes you have to be more than a scientist. You have to let nature take its course.'

I could see that the indecision was back: Danni the scientist, or Danni the caring, loving woman I thought I'd lost.

'Come with me, please,' I asked her. 'Let's take that walk that I asked you about before.'

Paul stayed behind with the van, as we threaded our way through the midst of the kaleidoscope. I saw her studying the spectators, some of who were sharing their picnics with the insects. Some butterflies flocked to honey-smeared slices of bread, whereas others preferred saucers with rotting fruit brought especially for the occasion. Young children, teenagers and adults of all ages joined in the experience.

I think it was then that the girl I once knew began to gingerly emerge from that chrysalis where she hidden for all those years. Still, it was only when she saw the British swallowtail that her face lit up like a child's on Christmas morning. My own copper-haired butterfly had returned.

'It shouldn't be here yet it is. They live in Norfolk, England, because the larva only feeds on milk parsley and there's certainly none of that around here,' she explained in her best lecturer tones. Seeing my expression, she apologised. 'Sorry. I'm preaching to the converted. Will you forgive me?'

I took her hands in mine and kissed them. 'Always,' I replied.

As we sauntered along, Danielle reached over and clasped my hand in hers, swinging them back and forth in an exaggerated way. It was like old times when we had gambolled through the fields as children.

'Do you remember Jenny Simmonds? She's married now. Two children,' she told me. 'I've been thinking about having some myself. Never wanted to be involved in a relationship, though. Work was my life. But now, thinking about it, there's only ever been one man I loved, Adrian.'

'Me? Do you think we could try again?' I asked her quietly amidst the din of happy children. 'After all, we're both a lot older now.'

'It's a possibility,' she said, smiling. 'But right now, we have a decision to make about big blue, the not-so-extinct insect we have cooped up back in the van.'

When she returned, I knew what the decision would be: freedom for the Xerces blue. Hopefully she would find a mate and the next generation would be conceived. And maybe this kaleidoscope of butterflies would happen once again. Here or elsewhere, it didn't matter.

*

Six days later, Danni and I returned to Whitestone. She'd decided to take some leave from her position at the university.

While we ambled between the trees and vibrant wild flowers, she laughed and made daisy chains for us both. The butterflies had left; disappearing to wherever butterflies go. Obviously, there were a few still there and, despite cursory glances as they danced from flower to flower, we didn't see the Xerces at all.

'Aren't you the teeniest bit curious?' I asked her, brushing a hair from her forehead.

'About what?' she giggled, as we reclined on the lush grass in the clearing where we'd met. The summer breeze blew dappled shadows across our faces.

'The reason they came?'

'Oh, I worked that out, sweetheart. Science doesn't have the answers. It never did.'

I sat up, turning to gaze down at her smiling face. I was puzzled.

'Think about it. What happened that special day?'

'We found one another again?'

'Exactly. The kaleidoscope brought us together. Thousands of butterflies just for us.'

Were we that special? Was nature that generous to our future happiness? Still, it was as good an explanation as any.

I lay down by her side again, gazing up at the cloud-kissed sky. I squeezed her hand. 'Maybe you're right, Danni. Maybe you're right.'

White Horses

Sharron sat back against the willow tree. It was the only shade on the grassed slope overlooking the estuary and even here, the sun's heat was uncomfortable.

Gazing at the waves, she scribbled a phrase into her notebook. 'Neptune's children?' she thought, before dismissing the image almost as quickly as she had considered it. 'No, far too sickening!' She erased the phrase from the page before placing the pencil on her lips.

Sharron scanned the river beach in front of her. It felt relaxing. Overhead, the sun was still hot, although the late afternoon sea breeze made it more bearable. There were a number of people basking on the sands and rocks, many already burnt, not yet realising that fact. Elsewhere, families played their simple, fun games, barely aware of the woman beneath the solitary tree. Her gaze returned to the wind tossed waves.

'Rows of snow-capped hills…' She dismissed that thought as well.

'They're called white horses.'

Sharron turned her face upward to the male figure that was standing to her side. He was also looking at the river.

'Excuse me?' she said, conscious that she was seated in the shade and that he was standing. This made her feel slightly uneasy.

'The waves. My mum called them white horses, galloping over the water, chasing each other.'

Sharron turned to the river again, nodding in agreement. 'I can see why. Thanks. I've been trying to write something about them in my mind. I…I write a bit of poetry when I can.'

The man walked in front of her, his back to the sun. 'Mind if I join you?' He gestured, indicating the surrounding area, 'It's the only shade on the beach.'

'It's all right. I'm going now.'

'No! What I mean to say is, don't go because of me. I'd…I'd like some company.'

Sharron examined him through her sunglasses. He was dressed smartly in a crisp, beige shirt with slacks. Unlike herself, hiding behind the glasses, she could see his eyes clearly. He was young, about her age. Although the shirt was a loose fit, she could discern that he was well built…an athlete, perhaps?

She made her decision. 'Okay.'

He sat near her, although not so close as to make her uncomfortable. They remained quiet, content with their private thoughts while staring at the sunlit tableau before them. Upon the sands, a small boy was trying to kick a football. To his left were a number of rocks which were wet from the crashing water. Yachts drifted in the distance.

Sharron slowly turned her head towards the man. He was sitting on the grass with his arms clasped loosely around his knees. She recognised him now – he was an athlete and a famous one at that.

Before she could speak, he commented on the weather. It was a mundane statement. Sharron felt disappointed. She had hoped for some deeper insight.

He spoke again, as if reading her thoughts. 'My mother used to bring me here. We'd both lie watching the waves, then imagine we'd be riding them to far-off places. China was a favourite for some reason.' He paused for a moment and the wistful expression faded. 'She died when I was seven. After that…well, life was never fun again.'

'You seem to have turned out all right.'

'Yeah. My dad took over. Said he'd make a man of me.'

'And…?'

'He did!'

Sharron expected him to continue but he did not. She noted the angry undertone in his voice as he'd mentioned his father.

'By the way, name's Craig.'

'I know. I've seen you in the papers.'

The child with the ball was still playing. More often than not, his efforts left him missing then falling onto the sand. Both Sharron and Craig watched, drawn to the shrill screams of delight as the boy raced around.

'Guess you want my autograph?'

'No, thanks.'

Craig seemed surprised, so she continued. 'Don't bother collecting them.'

'Fair enough!'

Sharron glanced over to him. He was examining his hands, obviously embarrassed from her rejection. Craig Stirman, or 'The Starman' as the crowds called him. 'Football Superstar'? Or simply a guy with the same problems and doubts as she had? She usually avoided people when she was out by herself, preferring to hide in the shadows. Whatever the reason that she had stayed to chat with this celebrity, she had her own problems to resolve and listening to him wasn't helping her.

'You said you write poetry?'

'I'm a teacher. Poetry is only a hobby, though I've had a collection published last month. Only a small one but it's something I'm proud of.'

'That's great! I love poetry too. All sorts…Keats, Judith Wright, Dylan Thomas…'

Sharron eyed him quizzically.

'Yeah, me…a footballer who likes poems! Weird, eh? Get a lot of stick from the rest of the team, but I do enjoy reading them. Favourite's Robert Frost. Dad made me give it up at school yet I still love it. Helps me relax and focus.'

Sharron knew that she had the type of personality that people felt comfortable with. She was a good listener and it helped a lot of anxious people to have a receptive audience.

'I do all right at footy but sometimes I wonder…'

Sharron waited, considering if she should prompt him. She decided against it. Instead, she peered at the shadow edge in front of her. The setting sun was pushing the tree shade further up the slope, almost touching their feet. She'd have to move soon.

Suddenly Craig continued, his voice now even more pensive. 'I know you probably don't understand. Frost said it all in one of his most famous poems. Regrets about life's decisions in "The Road Not Taken". That's me, all right. I feel my whole life is football. My dad made me practise, practise, practise…all the time. School, then the club…' He scuffed the grass with his heel, watching it as though he expected some deep revelation. 'Now, I wonder if that's all that I am.'

They were both startled when a ball bounced in front of them before rolling to stop nearby. The boy was running towards them. Craig stood and carefully threw the ball back to him.

The child scooped it up eagerly. 'Thank you, mister,' he called out.

Sharron began to gather her few possessions – her bag and shoes. 'I've got to go,' she said, adjusting the huge sunglasses she usually wore when out by herself. She knew that other people were uncomfortable when they couldn't see her eyes, yet that was never her intention. The glasses simply gave her a sense of privacy, concealing her striking beauty from unwanted attention and comments. A paper bag might have been more effective to hide beneath but it certainly would be much more conspicuous than the sunnies.

Sharron took a last glance at her beach. She lived nearby and often came here. Something wasn't right with the scene.

'Craig! Where's that small boy gone?'

Craig stood up. 'Not sure! With his mum?' he suggested, scanning the beach intently.

'No, she's over there. She's searching for him too,' Sharron commented, pointing. She was beginning to be concerned. Suddenly, at the same instant, she saw the limp form on the rocks. 'Over there!' she called out, pointing.

Craig's reflexes and speed surprised her as they both dashed to the child. By now, others were coming, including the boy's mother.

Craig assumed control. The toddler seemed to have fallen over some rocks. His face was under the water in a pool.

'He's not breathing,' Craig announced frantically. He eyed the onlookers, searching for some person who would step forward and announce that he or she was a doctor. Craig asked. No one moved.

'CPR!' he yelled to Sharron.

She nodded, moving slowly at first. The footballer told a woman holding her mobile to get an ambulance. In the midst of the gathering small crowd, Craig took a deep breath, concentrating on the task ahead.

'You do his heart. Not too hard, he's only little,' were his instructions to Sharron as she knelt over the boy.

For the next few minutes, both of them worked together on saving his life. His airways were clear but, as each second passed, their despair deepened. He wasn't responding. They could hear the child's mother crying, yet she stayed back, aware enough of the situation to allow these strangers to do their job. They were his only hope.

At last, the toddler gasped and spewed water from his tiny mouth. He took deep gulps of air before he tried to move. 'Mummy,' he sputtered as she cradled him. He seemed to be all right.

Craig and Sharron stood to the cheers of the crowd. Although Shannon had removed her glasses earlier in the rescue, it was only now that Craig noticed her eyes. They were an intense blue. They were also wet with tears of relief.

The ambulance came soon after. More onlookers had arrived and questions were asked by everyone including a middle-aged policeman.

After a while, Sharron wandered back to the tree at the top of the slope. Craig was following. The shadows had gone as the evening sunlight blanketed the area.

As they stood under the leaves, she turned to Craig. 'Does that answer your question?'

He seemed puzzled. 'Sorry? What question?'

'You wondered if being a footballer is all that you are. Remember?'

Craig paused, touching a hand to his chin, pensively. He smiled as he considered the answer. 'I guess it does.'

Sharron gave him a moment before continuing. 'Shall we get going to the hospital to see how he is? You said you'd give me a lift.'

Craig nodded and they began walking to where his car was parked. They stayed by the water's edge, their feet bare on the damp sands. However, within a few yards they were met by a group of teenagers.

'Autographs,' Craig sighed. 'At least someone wants my signature. It'll only take a minute or two,' he said apologetically to Sharron.

Although he readied himself for the group of teenage girls, they ignored him to converge on Sharron. Quite a few were clamouring for her attention. She grinned at Craig, whose face was a mixture of shock and surprise. His features did not change when they began chatting about their holidays and adventures. Some of her class. One even had a book of poems she asked Sharron to autograph. Craig noticed that Sharron's photo was on the back cover.

After the group had left, Sharron giggled. 'Sorry. They're not into football. Not everyone is, I'm afraid.'

'Guess I deserved that. So, tell me…why the giggles?' Craig enquired.

'You,' she laughed. 'Your expression was absolutely priceless.'

'Yeah,' Craig smiled as he recalled his shock at being ignored. 'Sometimes I need reminding that I'm not the biggest starperson around.'

They stopped to watch the sun setting on the horizon. After a minute, Craig reached out to touch her fingers, which she willingly intertwined in his. The sunlight glistened on the water as they both gazed at the waters.

'The white horses have gone,' Craig commented.

'It's okay. They're not far away. They're resting in their seaweed meadows.' She knelt down to put her hand into the waves lapping on the beach.

Craig knelt also, placing his hand on hers. He closed his eyes. 'Yes, I can see them now. They're sleeping…dreaming.'

Sharron rested her head on his shoulder. 'And what do they dream about?'

Craig's answer was thoughtful, his mind drifting back to similar conversations with his mother. He concentrated. 'Why, thoughts of another day when they can gallop freely with their friends.'

Sharron closed her eyes also. The gentle sounds of lapping nearby merged with the quietness of dusk. She was almost afraid to ask him, fearing that this magical moment would be shattered but she had to know. 'And…and will we be here again tomorrow to see them? You… and I, together?'

Craig paused for a moment before kissing her gently on the cheek. His voice was a soft whisper in her ear. 'Oh, yes. White horses couldn't keep me away.'

The Meerkat Conspiracy

'Over there, Rhonda! It's another one! The little beggars are every-where!' Dad exclaimed, pointing at the garden display. 'And that one even lights up at night!'

'Calm down. And watch your language. Little ears?'

He looked down at six-year-old Chloe by my side.

My father continued to vent his anger, although he was now more subdued. He knelt down next to Chloe. 'Sorry, precious. It's just that those meerkat thingies are all over the place these days.'

'But I love them. They're so cute. I have them on my slippers. Or I did have before Goldie ripped them up last week.'

'Dog's got good taste,' Dad grumbled to himself as he stood and resumed shopping.

He had asked us along to help choose new furniture for his living room. The old lounge suite and furniture were apparently dirty and torn. Suddenly his eyes glared angrily once more as he half-ran to another display.

We followed more slowly, holding hands. Other customers were beginning to notice my father's unusual behaviour.

'For heaven's sake, Rhonda. A meerkat Mona Lisa! Rembrandt would be turning over in his grave!'

'You mean Da Vinci, Dad,' I corrected, never sure when he was winding me up about his memory.

Sadly, he was right about the picture. A furry beast, dressed as the iconic lady, peered back at me. The enigmatic smile was gone, replaced by a stupid grin.

Throughout the shopping centre, we'd witnessed all manner of meerkat merchandise: school books with matching pencil cases, posters, radios, cutlery, clocks. No wonder Dad was upset. Their song had been number one for five weeks now. I wondered if, in thirty years' time, anyone would admit to buying it. Memories of 'Agadoo' sprang uncomfortably to mind.

My husband, Jason, even had one on the sat nav. He claimed it was for Chloe. However, I knew the truth. I'd seen him smiling every time he heard the squeaky falsetto voice saying, 'Turn right in two hundred metres, you silly human, you.'

Ten years before, most of us had never heard of the 'giant rats' as Dad called them. Now they'd infiltrated our society as insidiously as a flu bug attacks our bodies.

Dad saw my face grimace as I noticed shampoo bottles adorned with the African mammals and labelled 'Meerkat Fur and Whisker Wash'.

'You know I'm right, don't you, Rhonda?' He placed his tanned hand on my arm but I couldn't look him in the eyes.

*

Later, as we sat on the park bench, Chloe was playing ball with our Labrador. There was a Miss Fluffy ice cream van parked nearby, although neither of us fancied the new animal-shaped choc ice proudly displayed on the van window.

In an attempt to take Dad's mind off his fixation, I chose to chat about how he'd been doing on his computer course at the local college. He'd wanted to expand his knowledge about social media and had even joined up to some sites. I wondered if he was interested in dating organisations. After all, it had been four years since Mum had passed away.

He answered me politely, even commenting about the video posting site that Chloe had shown him where babies pulled faces or ordinary people did funny things by accident. He'd seen quite a few of her favourites when he'd babysat the previous week. Sadly, though, our conversation soon returned to his pet obsession of the moment.

'Did you hear the latest? The PM has adopted one as a mascot for parliament and is actually encouraging them to be sold more and more as pets. Of course, animal behaviourists state that this isn't a good idea. Digging up your front room isn't the sort of thing most people would tolerate.'

I didn't know that news, although I wasn't surprised. For the next few minutes, I simply sat quietly, watching Chloe and our dog, Goldie, enjoying themselves.

After a while, I asked my father why they were everywhere. Was it an advertising gimmick gone mad or was there perhaps something else…something more sinister?

Dad answered calmly. There was no danger that his memory was vanishing; he was still as sharp as ever. 'I've been studying them, you know – the real animals that wildlife gurus like Attenborough introduced to television audiences a decade or so ago.'

Goldie wandered over to our bench to flop down at our side. She was tired from stick-fetching, not being as young as she used to be. We watched Chloe on the swings with two of her schoolfriends.

My dad dropped into his professor mode even though he'd retired some years earlier. He'd made a name for himself in the study of sound waves. 'They're highly intelligent social creatures, mainly insectivores, but they'll eat mice, spiders and plants. Four litters a year, three pups in each litter, and they can live to fourteen years of age in captivity. I've watched them foraging for food. One always stands guard then swaps over after an hour.'

'Seems like a soldier on sentry duty.'

'Exactly. Organised and disciplined. Very adaptable too. They've even got their own language; special high-pitched whistles telling the others, it's safe, eat, play or panic – extreme danger. I did some recordings, myself.'

He paused, unsure if I were ready to hear his conclusions. 'I…don't laugh at this, Rhonda. I believe that they're trying to ingratiate themselves into our society. When we discovered them, they discovered us. Life as a pampered pet is much better than struggling against predators in a desert, you know.'

Dad sat back waiting for my reaction. I didn't laugh. I'd already heard that breeders had modified their destructive behaviour patterns…or maybe it was they who were changing to avoid alienating the people who would shelter and feed them. It wouldn't take much to become more family friendly. After all, they weren't much different to rabbits and how many homes had one of those?

'They'll learn and they'll continue with their…their propaganda. We won't be able to resist those endearing faces for long, and then? A damn giant rat in every household! Mark my words,' he added finally.

Goldie nuzzled my hand and I automatically stroked her fur. She stood up and padded across to sit by another dog and her human family. We waved to them. There was no problem, as the dogs knew one another and usually met each day when our friends and we came with our kiddies. It was a rare public space where dogs were permitted without leads.

'I wonder about that dog sometimes, Dad. She's a part of our family and Chloe loves her to bits. I guess I do too. I swear at times she listens to us, like just now.'

'What's that got to do with the meerkat problem, sweetheart?'

'Nothing, I guess. Just patting Goldie made me think of pets in general,' I explained.

'You do realise that dogs were once wild animals, like wolves, maybe fifteen thousand years ago. Them, and cats. They've been a part of civilisation for some time now and I reckon might be a bit put out about sharing us with the giant rats too.'

Goldie walked back to us, lay down and closed her eyes.

Dad leant over to talk to her. 'Well, Goldie, what have you and your furry friend been discussing? The weather? The canned food you ate last night? The meerkat invasion?'

At the last question, Goldie's ears pricked up, her eyes opened and she licked her lips.

I gazed around the park. It seemed like each family or couple had a dog with them. In addition, there were millions of cats living the life of Riley in households around the country as well.

Inadvertently, Dad had realised the truth: the meerkats might have plans to slowly invade our homes, but our existing pets would definitely have their own plans as well. I recalled a change recently that my cousin, Paige, had pointed out: cats and dogs weren't as aggressive towards one another any more. In fact, in our household, Goldie and our moggie, Tiger, were actually sleeping together. I'd put it down to their ages and familiarity. However, the same thing was happening with our other friends' pets also. Had the age-old antagonists called a truce to present a united front against a new enemy?

I faced my father and smiled. 'I don't think mankind has anything to fear from your meerkat conspiracy, Dad. Don't get me wrong. You just might be correct about how they're trying to become closer to us. It's simply that I suspect it won't be long before those usurper giant rats of yours will lose their moment in the limelight. A rumour about exotic diseases, some bad publicity, perhaps? No one will discover who, or what, started it but the only meerkat merchandise people will see in the future will be in car boot sales or more likely rubbish tips. And as for those little animals becoming the latest must-have pet, it will never happen.'

Dad and Goldie exchanged a knowing glance. 'I believe you're right there, sweetheart. Mum always said you could see the big picture. I feel a whole lot better.'

At that moment, I received an SMS from my cousin, a website she wanted me to look at. I was about to close my phone when I saw the dreaded 'M' word in the address link. I opened it up and watched the gripping video for three minutes. I could not believe what I had just seen. The caption simply said 'Meerkat playing'. Paige said that it gone viral (whatever that meant) – over four million hits in the last nine hours.

Shaking a little, I viewed it again. The destruction of someone's home by one single meerkat was shown in all its frightening terror. The tiny mammal was manic, ripping the lounge suite to shreds, attacking stuffed toys and dolls then smashing cupboards into pieces. All of the time the creature was screeching like a demented beast. I sat there in silence, horrified at the sight. What if there were a child in that room? It was only at the end of that second viewing that I recognised the room which had been trashed.

'Dad?'

He shrugged. 'It was only a matter of finding the right ultrasonic frequency, Rhonda. That one I chose was the equivalent of "Go on and play. Really enjoy yourself. Do whatever you want." No one was hurt and the giant rat was fine afterwards, although she was a bit tired. I don't think she'd had so much fun in her entire life.'

He stood up nonchalantly and patted Goldie on her head. 'Now what would you and Chloe say to an old-fashioned ice cream cone? My treat. I'll even stretch to a chocolate thingy inside them as well.'

Chloe ran over to us, having heard the magic mention of her favourite sweet. 'What about Goldie, Granddaddy? Can she have one too?'

'I'm afraid not, young Chloe. Doggies shouldn't eat ice creams. They're not good for their tummies.'

I glanced over to my father, considering the last few minutes. He and Chloe turned towards me while Goldie sat obediently awaiting my reaction.

'No problem,' I said, reaching into my handbag. 'I've got a special treat just for our Goldie. Come here, girl.'

Her eyes lit up and she began to salivate as I threw to her the meerkat-shaped doggie chew that I'd purchased yesterday. Between mankind's dogs and cats, along with my dad, the little beggars wouldn't stand a chance!

Treat or Trick

'I'm ready, Mummy.' Mandy Brookfield was so excited. Her first proper Halloween.

Her mother, Doreen, knelt in front of her beautiful little girl, adjusted the black pointed hat and kissed Mandy on the cheek. 'You look gorgeous. Even I'm scared. Have you got your wand?'

Mandy brandished the silver stick with a flourish and lifted the makeshift tiny broomstick with its spray of twigs. Her mother was dressed in a matching black outfit with cape and hat. Their pointed noses and gnarled green-tinged skin completed the picture. The witching hour had arrived.

Mandy loved her costume and was so pleased at the reactions when she knocked on doors and was given special treats. As they wandered down the streets of their leafy suburb, Doreen watched the assortment of beasts, zombies and fairies who ran excitedly up to front doors, called out 'Trick or treat', then collected the usual confectionery treat that was offered. Proud parents watched their little creatures protectively.

'Hi, Helen,' Mandy called out to a skeleton who was approaching

'Is that you, Mandy? Cool costume. Are those warts on your chin?'

Mandy blushed.

'Just some special make-up,' Doreen explained.

'You got lots of sweeties,' Mandy said admiringly, looking in Helen's painted bony basket.

After chatting for a moment, they went in separate directions.

'Helen''s nice, Mummy. She doesn't call me names like some of the others.'

Doreen knew about the bullying and had been to the school to try to resolve it. The worst culprit was a horrible, spoilt brat called Sean, thought

Doreen. She realised that Mandy had problems. What child didn't? Still, she hated the nickname that Sean used all the time; 'Mixed-up Mandy', just because her little girl confused things like left and right. She was only seven, after all. Doreen's smile faded for a moment then she remembered her daughter and this special night for them both.

Doreen recalled her own childhood. So much had changed over the years. Now she felt so repressed at hiding who she was from the world. Hopefully, Mandy would grow up with a better feeling of self-worth. If only Sean would stop picking on her.

They decided to cut across a park. Lots of other excited kiddies and parents were rushing by them. Suddenly she sensed a change in Mandy's demeanour.

Her daughter clutched Doreen's hand tightly. 'It's Sean, Mummy.' Her voice was quivering.

Doreen saw him too, dressed as Frankenstein's monster. Doreen had a fleeting thought of how appropriate his costume was.

As Sean and his mother approached, Doreen could hear his raucous voice. And then, when he noticed the two of them, he became even louder.

'Look, Mum. Two ugly witches. It's Mixed-up Mandy under that mask. She told the class that she'd be a witch tonight. Mixed-up Mandy! Mixed-up Mandy!' He yelled, taunting Doreen's precious daughter in front of her.

How brazen of him, and Sean's mother simply watched, saying nothing to chastise her obnoxious son.

Mandy was starting to cry. Her special night was ruined.

'Will you tell your son to stop insulting my daughter?' Doreen demanded.

'It's only a bit of fun. Besides, they're children. No harm done,' was the glib reply.

At that moment, Sean was in Mandy's face, continuing to harass her. He reached up to poke her face and drew back in shock. 'Mum. It's not a mask. Or make-up. She really looks like that.'

His mother bent down to look, then stared at Doreen too. Quickly she reached out and tugged at the tuft of hair sprouting from a wart on Doreen's nose. Doreen cried in pain and shock. Their secret had been discovered.

'Wha… What are you two?'

'Maybe they really are witches?' Sean suggested.

It was then that Doreen struck them with a paralysis spell. She was so angry. She looked around the dusking parklands. The other trick and treaters had gone home. They were alone.

Doreen was livid. 'One night! One lousy night each year when we can take off our concealment spells and wander the streets without a disguise. Now you and your foul-mouthed son have ruined it all. What can we do with you?'

Being paralysed, neither Sean or his mother could answer.

'Transform them, Mummy.'

Doreen considered it. Two more missing people to add to her list? There would be a little fuss but nothing major.

'Yes,' she said, rummaging in her purse for some mar marian leaves and dragon blood resin. She added some other ingredients and sprinkled it on the grass.

'Can I do it, Mummy? I've been practising.'

Doreen nodded. 'Something gross and slimy please, Mandy.'

'I know… 'Myrrh, myrtle, and wolfsbane, Turn these people to toads of cane.'

Doreen had been taking photos of her daughter's first incantation and so was distracted. Yet when Mandy raised her wand, Doreen screamed., 'No! You're holding the wand ba–'

But it was too late. In a puff of smoke, Mandy and Doreen were transformed, leaving Sean and his mother to run for their lives.

Mandy looked up at her mum. 'I'm sorry.'

Doreen swore. The cardinal rule of witchcraft. Never point the wand backwards!

'You said a naughty word, Mummy.'

Doreen continued to use naughty words as she hopped over to pick up the wand with her cane-toad leg. Perhaps she could reverse the spell but she wasn't hopeful.

Mixed-up Mandy had struck again.

The Lady of the Lake

I could have called her the Water Lady, although I always preferred The Lady of the Lake. Maybe it was my fascination with all things to do with Camelot and King Arthur when I was young. I would have loved to have been Guinevere although, given my tomboy nature, maybe King Arthur was more my style.

To have our own version of mythology in our township appealed to my wish to live somewhere important. The truth was, in the early nineteen seventies, the valley didn't have much going for it.

I used to see her wandering along the lakeside or pottering around her run-down shack whenever I was coming home from swimming. I never could understand why she could live in the middle of the park that surrounded the lake. Generally, I left it till it was starting to dusk. I hated being home without anyone else there. Dad worked all day and Mum…well, she'd run off years before.

The Lady was about fifty, I reckoned. Really old. And she always seemed to be looking for something, in the rushes by the cool, water's edge or out there on the mirror image lake. She always wore the same grey tattered hat and coat, even when the evening air shimmered with heat from the sun. Sometimes I'd wave. She never waved back.

When I told Dad about seeing her, he looked at me strangely for a minute. He muttered something about me having special sight then told me to have nothing to do with her. I asked him why.

He simply said, 'Just stay away, Carol. For me.'

I understood that there were bad people but, back in those more innocent days, I never believed that there was any danger from those around where we lived. The evil folks lived elsewhere, like the criminals in the cities. I saw them on tele in shows like *Homicide* and *Division Four*. The valley was different; safer, slower, more serene. On the other hand, my dad knew best, so I diligently bypassed the Lady and her shack without truly realising why.

One afternoon, I was walking through the park with a bunch of fish in my net. My dad thought they were a treat, though I wasn't so keen. Too many yukky bits to remove when you cleaned them. I'd brought Scamp with me for a change. He was new to our family because Dad reckoned that I needed a pal and I was old enough to care for him.

It was a beautiful day, filled with the sound of bees and gossiping birds creating their own special din. The midges swarmed around us making the sky seem all spotted when you looked across the lake at the tangerine and rose sunset. Some sulphurs screeched overhead causing Scamp to decide to chase after them.

'Come here, Scamp,' I called out as I followed him across the dried grass.

When he stopped, I realised we were only yards from the Lady's house. She was standing there, looking directly at us. I was suddenly afraid. My dad's warning came back to me.

'Sorry, missus. He got off his leash.'

She bent her head, peering intently at my face. 'You ain't the one,' she said with a touch of sorrow, before turning away to walk towards the rippling waters.

I put the leash on Scamp's collar and cleared out of there, dead fast. Everything about her terrified me. I didn't tell my dad, worried that he might ban me from going down to the lake altogether.

From that point onwards, I made sure that I avoided going anywhere near the old woman's home. I'd noticed that she always stayed close to it. That's why I was surprised late one afternoon to find myself approaching it and her. It was weird because the last thing I remembered was being ill and in the local hospital.

There was a cool breeze skipping across the water. The bees were long gone, lost in the cycle of seasons. Leaden clouds enshrouded the horizon as a sun shower, crossed from the lake to chase the wind. I was lost, searching for something familiar, and that's why I was there.

'Excuse me,' I cried, when I saw her withered silhouette opening a broken gate. I felt confused, weak from the exertion of walking. My legs and arms were marked with scratches from brambles as were my bare feet.

She turned from her lakeside vigil then hurried towards me, concern etched on her weathered face. 'What's a matter, child? You look terrible. Let me help you inside.'

Her arms supported me, guiding me down the overgrown path and through the doorway. I collapsed onto an over-stuffed lounge, grateful to be with someone. My mind was a muddle.

She fussed around me with a warm blanket being placed over my own exhausted body to stop the shivering. Hot sweet tea and some spiced apple cake were brought to nourish me.

After a bit, she sat near me quietly until I felt the colour returning to my cheeks and the sense of drowsiness dissipate. Then I realised who I was with and heard my father's voice again.

'Don't be afeared, girlie. You is here for a reason. I understand that now. I realise you ain't her but somehow I believe that you can find her for me.'

It was at that moment I noticed there was something unusual about her hands.

'You have six fingers,' I said in surprise.

She immediately hid then under the folds of her dress. I was sorry that I had embarrassed her, so I apologised. Dad had taught me about not judging others because they looked a bit different. I was certain it wasn't why he'd warned me to stay away. That meant there was another explanation yet I couldn't decide what. She seemed gentle and kind.

I still didn't feel right inside, although I had to get back home to my dad. He'd be worried about me, especially since it was dusking outside.

The lady lit some candles, suffusing the room with a flickering eeriness as well as a loving warmth. 'What's your name, girlie?'

'Carol.'

'That's a fine name. Mine's Miriam. Can I show you some things? They're very precious to me. I keep them in a special place, a secret place. Normally I'd not show anyone but I feel I need to let you know. Just in case anything happens. You understand?'

I didn't understand, yet it seemed very important to her.

Outside, I could hear the sound of water lapping on the lakeside shore as the scent of night-scented jasmine wafted through the barely opened window. An owl hooted nearby. Dad would be worried for sure. However, a part of me felt that it was important to stay there with Miriam for a little longer.

She knelt on the wooden floor and gingerly prised some loose floorboards up before reaching below to retrieve an old biscuit tin. It was similar to the one I recalled Mum hiding her secrets in, like the letters from the man she ran off with. Dad had found them after she went. It made him cry, something I'd never seen him do before…or since.

Old battered biscuit tins were where we kept the things closest to our heart. I watched as Miriam brought one to me.

She sat by my side. 'Like I told you, Carol, you being here with me here, by the lake…it's like we is both being given a second chance. I… I understand you want to be with your family and, believe me, girlie, I mean to make sure you will. Afore you go, I'd like to show you these. If that's good for you, that is?'

I smiled at her. The gaunt features that I'd recalled from when I'd first seen her with Scamp were softer now. Perhaps it was the light from the candle she placed on the wooden table. Over the following moments, I felt her sadness and her affection as she told me of her daughter, the one she'd lost many years earlier. The photos were often faded and were brown and white. I guessed they were old.

'And this last one is my Gwendolyn in her favourite dress. It were the green of fresh September leaves. Don't she look pretty? I…I miss my baby child so much.' And then she began to cry, a cry that reminded me of the wind I'd sometimes heard as I'd scurried home from swimming.

I reached out to hold her hands in mine. They were so cold. Then I felt energy flowing through me as my thoughts became suddenly clearer. I realised Dad wasn't at home at all. He was with my ailing body in the hospital waiting for me to wake up. Somehow a part of me, possibly my mind or my spirit self, had wandered off, eventually finding someone familiar, The Lady of the Lake.

The Lady gripped my hands tighter, so tightly that I winced in pain. And then I was gone.

Bright lights filtered through my closed eyelids as I heard Dad's voice.

'She's waking up. I'll get the doctor,' some woman announced from my side.

I was so groggy.

'You're in hospital, sweetheart. I…we thought we'd lost you.'

As I opened my eyes, I could see he'd been crying again. He said lost me? Gradually, I understood he wasn't referring to me being near the lake at night. There was a tube in my arm and strange machines clustered around the bed.

Over the next week, I drifted in and out of consciousness until I slowly regained my strength and a comprehension of what had happened to me. Some sort of infection. My temperature had reached one hundred and four apparently, and I'd been hallucinating, talking to someone only I could see.

The nurse who had been there when I came round only seemed to be there during the night when I was mostly asleep. I called her Nurse Collins, as that was the name on her blue starched uniform. She lifted my arm to take my pulse one morning as I awoke before the early day shift took over. When I noticed her hands, I opened my eyes wide, recognising an image from my mixed-up dreams.

'Excuse me, but is your first name Gwendolyn?' I asked.

'Goodness. No one's ever called me that since my mother passed some forty years ago. I was only a girl back then. I hated the name. Much prefer Wendy. How did you know, Carol?'

I thought for a moment, before answering. 'I think it's very important to tell you but I want my dad here too. Could you please ask him to come straight away?'

Once Dad arrived, I sat myself up in bed and told them everything. They remained there in silence until I finished. Then we agreed that, although I was due to go home the next day, all three of us would go to the lake first.

Parking our old car as near as he could, Dad and Wendy assisted me through the park to the shack by the lake. I was watching the uneven ground as I didn't want to trip.

'Here we are, sweetheart,' said Dad.

I looked up. 'No. This can't be right. It's all burnt-out,' I exclaimed.

'It's been this way for decades, ever since my mother died in the fire. I was only nine at the time. I managed to get outside but she…'

Still perplexed, we gingerly walked inside. Fortunately the floor was relatively intact.

'There,' I said, pointing. 'That's the settee I sat on. And that's the cup I drank from.'

Everything was now charcoal burnt or broken, with silken cobwebs enlacing them.

'I don't understand.'

'You must have been hallucinating, Carol. Those drugs we were using to stop the infection…' Wendy put her arm around my shoulder.

'No. It was real. How else did I know your name?'

Wendy held her hand out. Six fingers, just like the Lady of the Lake. Wendy had explained me it was called polydactylism and that it was inherited. And then there were the photographs.

I moved forward and began to force the floorboards up. Dad rushed over to help. I reached into the hole and brought out the rusted biscuit tin before passing it to Wendy.

'I remember this,' she said. 'I came back after the fire searching for it but could never find it. I…I thought it had been destroyed.' Opening it, she exclaimed, 'Oh. That's me in my green dress. And this one's Mum. I'd almost forgotten what she looked like.' Tears filled her eyes as she bent down to hug me in gratitude. She was reunited with her Mum's treasures and, in a way, with her mother herself.

*

I've relived that period in my youthful life a number of times since we chose to come back here for a short holiday. It's hard to forget your childhood and the things that shaped your adult life.

Although my daughter, Nikki, has been here to visit her grandpa over the years, this is the first time I've brought her out here to the park and its lake.

We sit on the grass, just her and me. My hubby is with Dad but I wouldn't have wanted him with us anyway. This is a time for mothers and daughters.

'It's beautiful, Mum,' she comments as we watch the lake waters.

Later, we talk about the shapes in the clouds as we watch dragonflies and butterflies playing their dancing games in the cool zephyrs. I hadn't intended to tell her about the Lady of the Lake or about how she saved my young life, although I decide that this evening is the perfect time to do so. By the time I've finished, the sun is setting.

Somehow, Miriam had taken some of that mystic power she'd possessed as a ghost and shared it with me. While others had occasionally seen her haunting the place where she'd died in that fire, I was gifted with that special sight that made her seem as real as normal folks.

I realised that fact, months later, having never again seen her at the lake. No one did. As time went on, the local people forgot about the spectral woman in grey, yet I'm determined not to. And now, my daughter knows about her too.

When I ask her if she believes my tale, she says, 'Yes,' without hesitation. 'I felt the Lady kiss my cheek while you were talking.'

I smile. She shares my ability to sense the spirit world.

'Was it a lonely kiss?' I ask.

She tips her head on her side, pensively. 'I don't think so. It felt more like a mum's kiss.'

It's time to go. We wave goodbye to no one in particular. Maybe the Lady of the Lake is waving back or maybe not. It doesn't matter now, because a part of her is with me. With us.

I take my daughter's hand in mine. Like mother, like daughter. Forever.

Apple Blossom Time

Secrets. We all have them; everyone we ever knew, everyone we never knew. It was time to share one of mine; the darkest one of all. Even so, I was worried about being here once more. Sometimes the past is best left in the past.

I paused, gazing at the foggy parklands that surrounded us.

It's strange how the smell or sight of something can stir up recollections of times long ago. The scientists tell us that the smells of the past are the most evocative in triggering our memories. I sniffed the air for the scent of flowers yet there was nothing. Perhaps it was my age.

'What's up, Gran,' Jasmine said as we continued to wander around the extensive gardens.

'The apple blossom over there. Just remembering meeting your grandfather that first time.'

Jasmine gave me a sideways hug. 'You've never talked about him much.'

'Doesn't mean I don't think about him, sweetheart. We met on a cold September morning. His suit was the wrong size, trousers above his pale blue socks, but as soon as I saw him, I knew he was the one.'

'Love at first sight?'

'Not for Brian. He was scared of me, I think. To be fair, we'd chatted on the phone to arrange our rendezvous but you can't really tell much from a voice. He'd been given my details from some dating agency. I think I was the final one on their list and he was afraid I'd also tell him, don't call me again after our date.'

'What was he like back then?'

'Skinny, with chestnut-coloured hair that was unkempt and far too long. He waved when he saw me. I guess he recognised me from the dating bureau's photo. As he'd been waiting under the apple trees for me to arrive, his dark suit was dusted with pale petals. I'm afraid that I burst out laughing at the sight.'

Jasmine interrupted my recollections, pointing to a picnic table with two benches either side. 'Shall we sit down please, Gran? I know I'm younger than you but the bump complains when I walk too much. Besides, it's where we arranged to meet him.'

We were lucky; the bench was in the sun that had begun to burn the fog away. The seats felt dry.

I smiled. 'Kicking again? Just like your mum when I was expecting.'

The cool breeze was bracing. I was glad we'd both brought heavy overcoats. Yet the scattering of rainbow tulips helped remind us of the beauty of this place.

Jasmine settled down gingerly next to me. 'So, what happened? With the laughing, I mean?'

'He turned to leave, avoiding any glance at my face. I realised my rudeness, ran to him then gave him a hello kiss. It was totally against my upbringing. That's when he gazed into my eyes and understood.'

'Understood what?'

'That we were kindred souls, with the possibility of something special happening between us. When I brushed the blossom from his shoulders, we watched it float to the dew-covered grass like pink snow. Some passers-by tisked at such an open display of affection in public, though I didn't care. I felt free and alive for the first time in ages. It was only later that I understood why – it was the trees.'

'Sorry, Gran. You've lost me there.'

'Look around you, Jasmine. Those trees have been there for ages, stoic and unmoving. All through the winter they sleep, without a single leaf wafting in the winds, watching and waiting. Yet once a year, for a few unique weeks, they wake up and celebrate a renewal of life, putting on their most delicate attractive clothing to announce themselves to everyone and everything that can see. My life had been regimented until then, at home and at school. Even the clothing I'd worn was deliberately chosen to make me boring and dowdy.'

'I see now. The woman inside you was ready to break free and, for some reason, you'd chosen Granddad to be your guide.'

'If I could have carved a message on that tree of life back then, it would have been so simple: "Brian Scott and Wendy Peters… Forever"'. I'd hoped he'd feel the same. As we chatted, we discovered we'd both of us fallen out with our parents, him with his stepdad, me with my mum. We were both looking for someone to heal the hurt, I guess.'

Jasmine and I sat in silence, each with our own private thoughts. I took a moment to breathe in the wistfulness of that first day together until a nearby scratching brought me back. Jazz pointed as we both watched two squabbling magpies dancing across the grass. The only other sounds were birdsong and the breeze caressing the flowers and emerging foliage above us.

Eventually, I was gently nudged from my melancholia.

'Gran. I do realise we've talked a lot about this reunion. Are you still certain about doing this? It's not too late.'

'I owe it to him. Actually, I owe it to everyone, including you and your mum. All our lives could have been so much different…hopefully better. It's about time I tried to resolve some of the past issues. After all, I have a reputation to maintain.'

Jasmine grinned. Her mother always referred to me as 'someone determined to get her way'. In retrospect, that was a kind description. I remembered the younger me as being overly selfish. As for Jasmine, I could only wonder about her feelings: trepidation, concern for me, all those unanswered questions and hurt for her mother's childhood?

I stared at the freckled grass as wisps of gentle zephyrs stirred the fallen petals.

Decades of springtimes had barely changed the park landscape. How many lovers had met beneath these resplendent branches? How many promises had been made…then shattered?

'Is that him, Gran?' My granddaughter's voice was tinged with excitement.

'I doubt that I'd recognise him now, sweetheart. Forty-odd years does a lot to change us all…inside and out. Sadly, it's not him. Despite not sending any up-to-date photos, he did say he'd be wearing a blue fleece.'

'Oh,' she sighed before putting her glasses back on to better scan the meandering flower-edged paths.

'We had some wonderful times together – the joys of youth someone called them. We spent hours in this park, him reading love poetry to me, or simply talking about nothing and everything. We used to go rowing on the lake over that ridge, before they made it into another football ground. He was terrible at rowing so I had to help him. Somehow that didn't seem to matter back then.'

'So why did the two of you split up…if that's not too painful a question?'

I paused, sensing waves of anguish still fresh despite the years since we parted.

'Was it someone else?' she gently prompted, leaning closer to me.

'Yes. Someone rich. To a young person, raised in near poverty, marriage to money was a dream. Dining in restaurants with linen table-cloths, going to shows and parties with celebrities, fast cars. Sad to say it was too much of a temptation.'

Jasmine placed her gloved hand on mine. 'That was the finish, then? So much for the fairy tale romance.'

I laughed. 'Relationships are much more tenuous with your generation. Go out with a boy one month then…how do you put it… "text-dump" him and move on. Back in the olden days, love was much more discerning…and painful when it ended. It was only after we broke up that I discovered I was pregnant. By then it was too late for us. He'd moved on and, although it was more difficult for me, I had to as well.'

'How sad. And how dreadful for you, having to raise Mum by yourself. I know it was more difficult back then. Mum told me stories.'

My change of expression must have hinted that I was upset. It had been a struggle.

'Don't feel bad, Gran. Mum told me that it was difficult to make ends meet but that you loved her so much, it made up for the hard times. You should have told him.'

'Although I did try to track him down, he'd left our town. In truth, he'd moved according to his friends but I couldn't trace Brian Scott at all. Britain of all places, even though he'd often told me that he hated the cold. I had no way to contact him. Eventually, I gave up. Life was too hectic to deal with, being an unmarried mum and all, without adding more time or expense to finding him.'

And yet here I was, waiting for the man who disappeared from my life so long ago to walk back in. How stupid was that? Still, I had to try to reconcile the past.

I reached out for Jasmine's gloved hand. Like me, she preferred the subtle feel of leather. 'Jazz, whatever happens here today, I want to thank you for finding my Brian and arranging this.'

'I was lucky when I began doing some digging. When you told me that you'd been unable to trace him on the internet, I checked his birth records on a hunch. You once mentioned him having a stepdad. He'd actually emigrated under his birth name, Brian Diamondaris.'

'Funny he never mentioned that, but I guess back then children often took their stepfather's name for convenience.'

I was so grateful for her detective work. Now Brian and I would be together again. It was time to make things right.

'The miracles of modern technology, eh?' I said to Jazz. Once we knew his proper name, it had taken us only minutes to track him down in Manchester. Type a name, press a few buttons and suddenly he's back in my life once mo–'

We saw him, both of us at the same time. He was emerging from the final tenuous mists by the stream.

I gripped Jasmine's hand tighter. We stood as Jasmine waved. He waved back. His brown hair was grey now and receding from his forehead. Also, he was limping. Nevertheless, I could still recognise Brian…my dearest Brian.

It seemed to be ages until he slowed then stood before us. His eyes showed the lines of age but his smile still reminded me of that nervous lad of our youth. 'You've not changed, Wendy. Still beautiful and still wearing pink.'

I began to protest that I wasn't wearing pink this time. Then I noticed the apple blossom on my grey woollen coat. I smiled back.

'Jasmine. Why not mention it? I must look a mess.' I berated her, playfully. Her own clothing was petal-free. Obviously, I'd been the only one sitting under the tree.

Then I remembered that introductions were in order. 'Brian. This is the lovely young lady who contacted you on the internet. Jasmine…' I took a deep breath. 'Your granddaughter.'

Seeing the abject shock on his face, I instantly regretted not waiting until we'd had a chance to greet one another properly. Jasmine helped him to a bench on the other side of the wooden table.

'You could have told me at the time, Wendy,' he eventually said. I could sense regret rather than anger. 'I would have stood by you, helped you… I would have married you in an instant.'

'Hold on. You left Gran for someone else.'

'No, Jasmine,' I explained. 'You misunderstood. Although I was certain we loved one another, I wanted more. I left Brian for the son of a company boss…a lad who wasn't who I thought he was. By the time I saw through his lies, your grandfather had left the country and, I'm sorry to say, I broke his heart.' I began to sob. 'I was the villain of the story, Jazz.'

'Villainess,' Brian corrected without thinking.

Despite the situation, I had to laugh. I wiped my eyes. 'You always were pedantic when it came to the English language, Brian.'

He stood to move towards me.

I pushed myself to my feet to hug him closely. 'For what I did to you all those years ago, I'm so truly sorry,' I told him contritely.

'But I'm here again, with you, Wendy. Thanks to this delightful young woman whom I dearly hope to get to know so much better. It seems we have much to catch up on.'

'Forty-six years.'

'And three months, two days,' he added. 'I never forgot you. Perhaps we could try to make up for those lost times?'

'I'd love to try but more importantly I want to see what the future will bring us…together. I can see I have my work cut out for me, though. Look at the state of your trousers.'

Brian grinned and his entire face and eyes lit up. 'What can I say? I need a woman's touch in my life. Now, might I suggest we find somewhere warmer? I feel the cold more these days.'

'Shall we all go to my place? There's someone there. Your daughter, Jasmine's mum, is waiting to meet you. She's…she's been waiting a very long time.'

'She could have come with you here.'

'We thought three women might be too intimidating. Didn't want to scare you off.'

'No chance of that, Wendy. But right now, I am a little apprehensive, seeing the daughter I never knew I had. You're the family I always wished I had and I see I'm going to be a great-grandfather too.'

'You already are – a little boy who's at nursery. His name is Brian.'

The Other Things

The Day Leeton Vanished

Leeton disappeared this morning. Agreed, it was only for a few minutes around two twenty but the entire place and some surrounding countryside went missing. More strange, if that's possible, was that their clocks and watches had lost time when it popped back into existence. It was as though the city and all its inhabitants had been frozen while they were gone.

'I still say no one would miss it if it had disappeared for an entire week, boss. It is Leeton, after all.'

I ignored Trevor's flippancy. He was the newest member of my investigative team and I'd seen the same horrified expression on his face as the inhabitants we'd interviewed this morning. Leeton, Goulburn, in fact any town or city, phasing into oblivion from Australia then reappearing, was a major concern to our government. That's why the minister woke me up at three-thirty and ordered all of us to, in his words, 'fly out and find out what the hell is happening'.

My name is Cindy Blackthorne. I doubt you've heard of me. I'm a…well, let's say I'm a problem solver. Even though I'm not all that bright, I sort of think sideways or laterally. There are reasons for all the weird things that happen in the country and it's my job, sorry my team's job, to solve the unsolvable. Our unwritten motto is 'Life Isn't Meant to Be Easy'. Apparently, someone important came up with the phrase in the past and we've adopted it.

My phone rang. No prizes for guessing who.

'Hello, minister. The copter's almost back at the shed. Most of the team are still at Leeton but there's been two more vanishings and we need more personnel.'

'You'll have them. Queanbeyan winked out two minutes ago. Twelve square kilometres of it.'

My body temperature felt like it dropped to zero. My daughter and my husband lived there. The rest of the team heard the conversation. Many of their families and loved ones lived there or in Canberra. This was personal now.

Luckily for us, Phil was piloting the copter, otherwise we might have lost control. Phil was the team rock. Almost nothing fazed him.

'Cindy? Are you there?'

'Yes, minister. My family...I'm...I'm okay now. I can see the affected area coming into view. It's huge. Like a shimmering haze. It's irregular. Cameras?'

Gina punched up a magnified view. 'Are you seeing this, boss? It seems to be farmlands. A tiny village. Cattle, horses. Is that a Model T Ford?'

'They're not moving. Spectroscopes and sensors suggest early twentieth-century atmosphere inside the barrier.'

My team were on top of it.

'Minister, it seems as though the satellite images of Leeton were correct. There's some sort of time displacement. Leeton, some of the countryside around Griffith, then around Narrandera, now Queanbeyan. They've all swapped time places, one after the other. Each time, they disappear for longer. Queanbeyan should return in...'

'Eight hours, forty-six minutes...'

'Should?'

'There's a sequence for the length of time they vanish.'

There was silence from the other end of the phone.

'There's panic already, Cindy. Financial markets...talks of terrorism. What if it hits Canberra? Melbourne?'

'We need to find out what started it all. Fortunately, no one's been injured, even those on the boundaries. It's as though they can pass through if they're caught in the middle. Cars, livestock. Then they're frozen like the rest if they're going in or are perfectly fine coming out.

Houses, utilities, no damage either. It's as though everything shuts down near the vanishings.'

By this time, we'd landed at the edge of the phenomenon. Hundreds of people rushed towards us in panic. While most of us went to examine the barrier, the commanding tones of Phil were broadcast over speakers, calming them down and allowing us to do our respective jobs.

The minister was on visual now, seeing the situation by video link.

'What's that smell?' I asked. The air reeked of it.

No one else offered an answer, although I knew that odour, recognised it from my past. And it was important. It was a pity my memory wasn't great for odours.

'There's a link somewhere,' I told him. 'Something happened at nine twenty a.m. somewhere near Leeton. The vanishings have been moving out from there. I need the Cray supercomputers allocated to my team.'

'How many?'

'All of them.'

'No. That's not possible. There's contracts and…'

From behind the minister another figure appeared on my screen. I recognised him.

'You're the woman who solved that nationwide food poisoning incident, last year?'

'Yes, sir.' When the country had panicked and no one could find the link, I'd discovered it. It wasn't the food or drinks. It was the contaminated containers and cutlery. Like I said, lateral thinking.

'You embarrassed a lot of important people then, Mrs Blackthorne. But you saved hundreds of lives. All the Crays, you say?'

'Yes, Mr Prime Minister.'

'Done.'

*

By the time Queanbeyan reappeared, we were up and running. Every single bit of information we had for the disappearances and what had happened beforehand to cause the first was being sifted through to find the link. It had to be natural…or supernatural. Nothing man-made could cause this.

I allowed myself a few hours to grab some sleep and see my family. They were unharmed by the vanishing, disappearing in the morning and appearing some eight hours later. They knew nothing apart from losing that time. It was as though the city's populace were fast forwarded those eight hours, from afternoon to late evening.

April was impressed, riding in the police car that rushed them from home to our base in Canberra, the so-called Shed.

I hugged them both tightly when they were escorted in.

'You're in charge of all of this?' Danny said incredulously.

My small super team of two dozen specialists had now grown to over eight hundred, with more coordinating the various computer links between the Crays.

'I don't want to go disappear again, Mummy,' said April. She was only three.

How could I reassure her when I didn't yet understand the cause? Moments after Queanbeyan reappeared, a section of the Kosciuszko National Park had vanished. This time, we estimated it would be gone for thirteen hours fifty-two minutes. It gave us some breathing space. No one wanted to lose a major population centre again.

'Any ideas, sweetheart?' Danny asked, half watching replays from cameras showing Queanbeyan being replaced by, we assumed, an earlier version of the area. Presumably, modern Queanbeyan had swapped places in time with the post-Federation settlement we had videoed. Tests showed it was 1913 and the Kosciuszko park swap was to the same year as well.

I was still half-asleep. I needed more but this crisis was now my responsibility to solve. The list of things that happened during the night was mind-blowing: changes to the power grid, astrological alignments, tidal changes, highway diversions.

The Crays were sifting through it, searching for correlations and I'd briefed everyone what they should be searching for. April was watching the myriad screens on the action room wall. I was holding onto April too tightly and she was squirming around, fascinated by the scenes on the screens.

'Magic,' she said. 'Like the bunny wabbit and the magicyian at my birthday. Do you remember, Mummy? Abrikadabri. Poof.'

'Shush, April. Mummy's trying to concentrate.'

Danny leant down to scoop her out of my arms.

'Hold on, Danny. What did you just say, sweetiekins?'

'Abrikadrabi. I'se sorry, Mummy. I be quiet now. Promise.'

'It's all right, darling. Mummy loves you.'

'And Daddy too?'

'Of course. Daddy too. But Mummy's got to go now.'

I kissed them both before they were led away. Out of the mouths of babes…

'Listen, everyone. Forget science and time travel machines. There's magic involved.'

Professor Dane Richmond wandered over nonchalantly. 'Magic?' he whispered. 'Are you mad? We're scientists, Cindy. What makes you think…?'

'The smell at the vanishings. I just recalled where I'd smelt it before. The dagger, Carnwennan.'

'The dagger used by King Arthur? It actually exists?'

'Yes. It was presented to our government as a gift when Federation happened in 1901. Our scientists discovered how to unlock its power twenty years ago. We haven't told the Brits, though.'

'Power? It's not being used in the Pinjar power station in Western Australia, is it?'

I was impressed. Only two dozen people knew the truth but Dane had guessed. I'd chosen the best people for my team and this had confirmed it.

He explained in a whisper. 'The figures never added up. That much power should use twice the fuel. Something to cover up in the future, perhaps?'

Dane turned to the team once again. 'Everyone. Please listen. Whether you believe in magic or not, it does exist. I want maps of all the leylines in Australia cross-referenced with any activity before the first Vanishing.'

'Excuse me, boss. What are leylines?' It was Trevor.

Dane answered him. 'Lines between places of power. They're supposedly lines of mystical energies like feng shui. In the past, that's where there's been sightings of ghosts, fairies and UFOs. The Aboriginals call them *turingas* or songlines.'

'Oh. Like through Uluru and Stonehenge?'

I nodded. Trevor was young but he would fit in perfectly with my team of like-minded scientists.

Within twenty minutes, we had our shortlist. One place sprang out immediately to four of us. The Murrumbidgee River. There had been a diversion opened three minutes before Leeton phasing out two days earlier.

Clearly interfering with these magical lines of force screwed time up. The next question was what to do next. Every time a part of Australia reappeared from the past, another part would disappear. So if we restored the area on the Murrumbidgee to the way it was before the new slip road was opened, what would happen to the Snowy area? Would it be stuck in the past, frozen forever one hundred years ago?

I was telling the PM what we'd discovered when all hell broke loose behind me.

Dane came running up. 'Problems, Cindy. Big problems. People in the areas that have vanished and returned: some of them are lapsing into comas. So far it's only been a dozen from Leeton but what will happen when it catches up with Queanbeyan?'

I excused myself from the conference call. Until then, no one had been injured from the vanishings yet that had changed. Some sort of delayed reaction. Lord. What if it affected Danny or April? I rang home straight away.

'Is everything all right, Danny?'

'Yeah. Why shouldn't it be? April's watching cartoons and…hold on. I heard a noise.'

I waited. Someone at the door? Another blinking insurance salesman?

'You there? April…she's behaving funny. I have to ring an ambulance, Cindy. Bye.'

Damn. It was happening. My little girl. Focus, Cindy. Your daughter needs you to sort this out. They all do. The whole country. Danny will do what he can but you have a bigger responsibility. The trouble was my body wouldn't listen to my logical mind. My daughter…my lovely April was in trouble and I needed to be there with her.

Gina came up to me as I began to go into meltdown.

'It's April. She's…'

She hugged me closely until I could push my little girl's crisis to the back of my mind. I was her best chance but I needed to be more than a mother now.

'Gina, we have to destroy the river diversion and restore the ley-line's integrity. But we have to do it between disappearances. There's a fifty-five-second gap between an area reappearing and the next vanishing. You need to set it up. I'll be on the other end of the phone. Keep me up to date.'

'Where are you going, Cindy?'

'Nowhere. I just need to make arrangements for April and Danny. Bring them here. We've the best medical facility in the area downstairs. I need to do this. Ten minutes.'

There were times you have to trust the team you've brought together. This was one of those times. By the time the Medevac helicopter had brought April and Danny to our facility, I'd managed to set everything in motion to restore normality to our country. Hopefully.

I stayed by April's side as we watched the televised operation taking place far away. My team were there, coordinating the arrangements. Explosives were set to totally destroy the diversion that had set off these vanishings.

I held April's tiny hand and prayed that all of those in comas would awaken when the vanishings ceased. Cameras were focused on the Kosciuszko National Park and a timer was also on the multi-screen display. I could see my team coordinating the operation at the Murrumbidgee. They were good. Better than that, they were brilliant.

'Fingers crossed,' I said to Danny as we turned our gazes to our small daughter lying in the bed.

This had to work. It had to. Modern medicine couldn't help her. At that instant, a long-distance picture of where Thredbo should be shimmered and we could see cars and shops once again. The digital clock started counting down as. Then, we waited, hardly daring to breathe.

A huge explosion ripped through the recently constructed diversion bank. I prayed that this would restore the natural mystic pathway of the leyline there. The river rushed back to its old course. Immediately, I heard April wake up.

'Mummy, I'm hungry.' Those were her first words. She was awake once more.

News came in within minutes from the satellite trackers. No new vanishings and the three hundred twenty-four coma patients from the vanishings were all conscious once again. I was certain that the government would present the country with a watered-down version of the truth and my team might have a minor mention for solving the crisis. That didn't matter. The most important thing was our daughter being well once more.

We stayed by her side all night, sleeping on the special beds set up in the ward. At eight o'clock, the minister rang for an update and to congratulate me and the team. I sensed there was something else, though.

'Cindy, I hate to ask this so soon after you've solved this little problem but we need your advice on a new matter. Four bright green wallabies have been captured in Tasmania. I don't suppose…'

Danny touched my arm. 'You go, sweetheart. We'll be fine. Go and save the world again.'

I smiled before kissing him. 'Give me two hours to get my team down there, minister. Four green wallabies, you say? How hard can that be?'

'It's a little more complicated, Cindy. They're all speaking French.'

I shrugged, already deciding which translator should come with us. After all, life wasn't meant to be easy.

Danni's New Pet

'Hello, honey! I'm home!'

Danni Jordan heard her husband's voice from the family room and was a little surprised. Not only was he early but she hadn't heard his car pull up in the drive. She stopped washing up the lunch dishes and walked briskly to join him. They had things to discuss.

'Where are you, Dave?' she asked when she couldn't see him in the room.

'Down here, sweetie. I've had a terrible day.'

Danni glanced towards the floor. However, she could only see a cat. It was black and white, one that she couldn't recall seeing around the neighbourhood.

'Here!' the cat said emphatically.

Danni saw his lips move and heard her husband's voice. 'But you're a cat! What's going on, Dave? Is this a joke?'

'No joke, my love. Anything but!'

Danielle knelt down to examine the animal more closely. Possibly it was one of those animatronic toys? She touched the fur. It was warm and it felt real to her.

'How?' she asked the feline, feeling a little silly as she did so. What if Dave were hiding somewhere, filming this for YouTube or something?

'Well, you remember that woman I had a blazing row with last week at work. The one I sacked without references?'

'Vaguely…the one you called an ugly, old witch?'

'Yeah. It turns out that she really was one…a witch, I mean. She came into my office this morning, locked the door and began shouting and throwing things around. After some time, she said she was going to have her revenge. She threw some foul-smelling powder over me and muttered some words – like a Latin incantation, I think. Next thing I know, there's a tremendous explosion and I'm lying in a corner of the room, only I'm not me. I'm a cat! This cat!'

'Go on. What happened then?'

'The office was destroyed. Furniture, bits of clothing, papers. It was chaos everywhere and the old woman…well, she was dead. Guess she overdid the magic potion or maybe her heart gave out. Only thing I know is all the staff at the office think I'm missing, possibly dead. Trouble is, they couldn't find my body. No one noticed a cat, lying in the rubble.'

'But you can talk. You could have explained, couldn't you?'

'No. I can only be heard by you, my wife, according to the batty old witch. Said you'd understand. She told me about her plans when she was gloating about transforming me. Not that I believed her until after she did it. I thought she was barking mad.'

Danielle was beginning to realise that, unbelievably, this was all true. She was now married to a talking cat. 'So why haven't the police contacted me?'

'Not sure. I suppose they're uncertain about the whole thing – magic explosions and all that. They've locked the whole office down – no one in or out, no phone calls. I imagine they'll contact you later.'

It was a lot for Danielle to take in. At last, she asked the tiny feline, 'So, how long will you be a cat?'

'Indefinitely, I guess. She said she'd change me back once I'd learnt my lesson but, now she's dead, I suppose I'll be a cat forever. May as well get used to it! After all, I still have you, my loving wife, to look after me, don't I?'

'I…I guess.'

'I can cuddle up on your lap at night, have you rub me under the chin, sleep all the time. Yes, I won't miss the old life at all. Actually, I fancy something to eat, now. I had to walk home from the office. I can't quite manage driving a car like this, can I?' Dave strolled over to the settee, jumped up and stretched out on a cushion. He licked his left paw and commenced to clean his furry face.

'Now, let's see. A lovely big steak, medium to well done, some cold beer, and I'd appreciate if you could switch on the telly – the sports channel. That's a good little wifey.'

Almost without thinking, she turned on the television and gave Dave the remote as usual. Danielle stared at her husband preening himself on her clean cushions. They'd be covered in cat fur in no time. As for Dave, human or cat, he was still the same.

At that moment, the front doorbell rang. Danielle went to answer it and returned with two police, who told her the devastating news. It appeared that her husband had been killed at work. Danielle began to cry and did her best to show the expected reactions of shock and remorse. All the time, Dave sat on his cushions at the other end of the room, occasionally switching channels as he watched the telly.

After the police had left, Danielle wandered over to her new pet.

'Ahem. Still waiting for that meal, sweetheart. Now would be a good time.'

'I…I'll have to nip out for some steak, Dave. Just put your paws up and enjoy the golf. I won't be long.'

She returned within half an hour and dutifully prepared his meal for him, even cutting it into bite-sized chunks for his little mouth. He'd drunk two saucers of beer before he announced, stretching his front legs above him, that he was feeling a little dozy and he fancied a tummy rub.

He was dumbfounded when Danni refused. 'I've given you a mild sleeping tablet with your meal, my darling husband. We're going for a little trip.'

'A…a trip?' Dave the cat said. He noticed that his speech was slurred and he couldn't move very well.

'Yes. I'm afraid your bad day has only just begun, my darling. Your witch friend came over to visit me this morning. She showed me details of your affair with your secretary, Linda. She even had some explicit video recordings. No wonder you were working late all those nights.'

'Linda…lovely Linda…I's can explain… S'not what you tink.'

'A bit late for that, my darling. We have an appointment with the vet. He's quite handsome and friendly. He and I have arranged to go out next Saturday night for a meal. I explained about how you were killed in the explosion today and he was ever so comforting when I started to cry.'

'But…why we's going to vet?'

'For your little operation, my darling. Can't have you wondering off to meet any girl cats in the evening, can we? And as for your future meals, forget the steak. I've found some cat food, specially for ones that have been neutered.'

Dave, the cat, felt quite ill. Danni was right. His horrible day wasn't finished yet.

Checking Out

Jenny Sandford looked in dismay at the long supermarket queue and sighed. Her shopping trolley was full, her feet ached and she'd had a hard day at work with some particularly obnoxious clients.

'There's a self-checkout that's free, madam,' a helpful, young manager suggested.

'Not one of those machine thingies? I get so flustered with them and, in the end, I have to call a person over anyway.'

'Our new upgrade is so much more person-friendly. Give him a try. You might be surprised.'

'Him?'

'His name's Kevin.'

Reluctantly, Jenny allowed herself to be guided over to Kevin.

'Hello, Mrs Sandford. How are you, this afternoon?' said an agreeable voice from the scanner.

'Er…I'm fine…Kevin. Thank you for asking.' Jenny replied.

'Lovely. May I call you Jenny?'

'I…I guess. But how do you know my name?'

'Camera. Facial recognition software. You shop here most Thursdays. Might I say that you appear to be a bit off-colour today. Relax, have a seat and take the weight off your feet. I'll scan all of your shopping for you.'

'Thanks, Kevin. I might just do that.'

Jenny watched as tiny robot arms reached out to extract the groceries, scan them on the barcode reader then pass them to other hands that carefully packed them.

A china cup appeared from the machine. 'Here's a cup of camomile tea.'

'How thoughtful. I love camomile. How…'

'I have access to all of your purchases from the past four years, Jenny. You always buy those delicious chocolatey oatcakes, too and… oh, excuse me, these desserts are almost out of date. I'll buzz a storeperson to swap them over.'

'Are you aware of my husband too? He comes shopping with me, although not very often.'

'Oh, him! I believe you could do better than being married to Steven.'

Jenny put her cup down, puzzled. She watched pensively as four boxes of cat food were scanned before being packed.

'Why would you say that?' she asked.

'Well, I'm not one to gossip. Forget I mentioned it, Jenny. Ah, here come the replacement desser–'

'Why did you say that about my husband?' Jenny's voice was much louder this time.

'Calm down, please. Your pulse rate is too high.'

'You…you're monitoring my pulse?'

'And respiration, pupil dilation. We always try to care for our customers at Super Duper Savers. Have another camomile tea, Jenny.'

'I don't want another blinking camomile tea. I want to find out why you dislike my Steven.'

'Please calm down. I'll tell you. However, you must sit down. I believe that Steven is being unfaithful to you.'

'My hubby? No way. He…he loves me.'

'I have proof, Jenny. He came in last Tuesday with a woman my memory banks identified as Anna Petrof.'

'Anna. They work together, that's all. Wait…last Tuesday he was interstate. Stayed overnight.'

Kevin's video screen sprang to life, showing Jenny's husband cuddling and hugging someone at the checkout. Worse still was the kiss: a very intimate one.

'They were purchasing two bottles of wine. New Zealand Shiraz. It was on special. Two for thirty-five dollars sixty… Sorry. You need a moment and I'm raving on.'

Jenny felt sick to her stomach. Regaining composure with an effort, she dried her tears. How could he?

A tissue popped out of a compartment followed by two others.

'I could offer you a whisky but you're driving,' the machine said. It had paused in scanning the groceries at this time.

Jenny absently assumed that Kevin must be fitted with some compassion chip as well as everything else. She was grateful for that.

She sat silently for a moment before deciding what to do. 'It isn't been the first time the little toerag has cheated on me, Kevin. But now, it will be the last. Might I please have a copy of that video?'

The checkout operation began again.

'Certainly. I never liked him after he kicked me in a delicate circuit board, saying I'd overcharged him. The video has already been downloaded onto your phone.'

'The joys of bluetooth connectivity,' Jenny mused. 'Don't suppose you're aware of any good divorce lawyers?'

The final few items were now being packed away.

'As a matter of fact, I do. Mrs Papadopoulos mentioned one only this morning. Just checking my data banks. Once her lawyer is finished, her "two-timing bathtub of a husband"' will be well and truly neutered…or words to that effect.'

Jenny winced. Would she want that to happen to Steven? The answer was a resounding 'Yes'.

'Could you download the lawyer's details, please?'

'Done. That will be one hundred and fifty-one dollars exactly, thanks. Cash or card?'

'Card please. Thank you for telling me about…you know.'

'As I said, you can do much better than him. You're very fit. Jenny.'

The young woman was shocked. 'I didn't realise you would think that.'

'I don't. My tastes run to appliances like that cute mint-green toaster over there. She's really hot. No, that "fit" comment was from Mr Newman, the manager who introduced us. He's single.'

'Is he now? Interesting,' said Jenny, checking out the young man two aisles over. 'I'll keep that in mind. See you next week, Kevin.'

'You too, Jenny. Who's next? Ah, Mrs Ritson. How's the arthritis today?'

Shushhh

I must be crazy; standing outside the door of the door of the woman who hates me most in the world. My mother had said I was invited for afternoon tea and, for some bizarre reason, I'd accepted.

My entire life has been a series of failures. Now I have no job, no home of my own, no friends, not even a cat. And I love cats. My mother suggested I stay with her when things went pear-shaped again, but we hardly speak. Old habits.

It had only been yesterday when Mother told me. 'No, I don't know why she wants to see you, Kerry. She hadn't spoken to me since Sharon died all those years ago. So it was a surprise to hear from her.'

I'd lain awake most of last night remembering Sharon's friendship, what had happened to her and how it was my fault.

As I huddled under the drizzling rain, I could hear Mrs Clark coming. This was going to be awkward.

'Come in from this dreadful weather, Kerry. I'm sorry for being so slow. Old age.'

An apology? For me? As I entered, I nonchalantly checked out the house. It was similar to Mother's, three houses away, but it was so gloomy, having tattered curtains shrouding the rattling windows. Dust covered the shelves and bookcase. Mrs Clark's appearance echoed her rooms. After Sharon's death and then her hubby's, she clearly given up, yet she'd made an effort today: a clean dress and some make-up, though it was clear that she hardly combed her silver-grey hair.

She ushered me into her dining room with two chintz-covered armchairs. The smell of freshly disturbed dust tainted the air.

'Sit yourself down, girl. I'll take your coat. Coffee or tea?'

Reluctantly I removed my coat. Even though I had no self-worth left, I could see her momentary glance of disapproval at my stretched clothing. 'Comfort eating' was the polite term some people used.

'Coffee, thank you.'

There were biscuits on the table – Monte Carlos, Sharon's favourite. Next to them was a pile of worn books. Diaries. Suddenly, I felt that apprehension return.

Returning moments later with a tray of hot drinks, Mrs Clark sat down opposite me. She smiled wanly. At least she was attempting to put me at ease.

'I decided it was time we had a proper chat, Kerry. I found Sharon's diaries in the attic last week. Of course, I realised they were there. Still, this time I chose to read them. There's a lot about the two of you and once I'd finished them, I understood why you were so close. It was something that's puzzled me for all of these years, even when she was alive.'

Sharon had kept diaries, after all. How much had she recorded about my secrets? I maintained an impassive face, despite drops of rainwater falling from my damp hair.

'Mrs Clark…'

'Jeanette, please.'

'Jeanette. Despite Sharon being six years older than me, she was my best friend. She helped me in so many ways. I was a difficult child…'

She laughed. 'Difficult? Kerry, no offence but you were a nightmare with your constant crying. Your parents, even the doctors, despaired. From the day Sharon first saw you in your crib, she was the only person who could settle you down. I can still recall her gently stroking your little head and saying, "Shushhh."'

I stared down at my clasped hands and bitten nails. 'That's the reason my mother and I never got on, I guess. Still, Sharon taught me how to be around other people and to…control myself.' I put the cup of coffee back on the table. 'Forgive my impatience, Jennifer, but how much was in those diaries?'

'I know why you screamed around people as a baby. It was their thoughts in your tiny head, thoughts that you couldn't shut out. You could read minds.'

I reclined back into the comfy chair. The truth was out. What next? Accusations of being a monster or a freak? Although Sharon knew, it had been my secret alone for the past seventeen years since her death.

'You have no idea, Jeanette. I couldn't make it stop for years after my birth. "What's for dinner? My feet hurt. I must pay the gas bill tomorrow. Why did he say that?" Then there were emotions. Men's were so intense. Sharon taught me how to gradually reduce the din until, by the time I was four, I could stop it altogether. She saved my sanity.'

I stood to wander over to a shelf where a framed photo of my dearest companion was proudly displayed. It captured her beautiful face, copper hair and dusting of freckles. Even those thick-rimmed glasses couldn't hide the sparkle in her eyes.

'This photo: when was it taken?' I asked.

'On her fourteenth birthday, two weeks before that drunk took my little girl's life.' Her voice quivered with the sadness of that loss.

I took my purse from a pocket and lifted out my own creased, photo of Sharon. I'd almost forgotten how vibrant she was. 'I miss her so much, Jeanette.'

Then, to my surprise, I felt a reassuring hand on my shoulder.

'Now I can see why you were so close. Guess I was jealous with her spending so much time with such a mixed-up child.'

'I was, wasn't I? So angry, so confused, so...'

'Gifted?'

'That's what Sharon told me. It's not a gift, though. It's a curse. Being assaulted by a barrage of jumbled thoughts.'

'But you did manage to touch a part of our thoughts that's ordered, didn't you? Our language. You learnt foreign languages simply by being near someone who knew them. I often wondered why the two of you would sit at the bus stop with that old Vietnamese woman. You were chatting in her native language that you'd learnt from her thoughts. No wonder she was so happy when she was with you.'

'Mrs Phan Tai. I'd almost forgotten her. One day, when I was four, Mrs Phan Tai was passing and I could hear Vietnamese from her mind. It was wonderful. And it didn't hurt me. We…we learn words then put them into what I call habit centres. When we need to express ourselves, we simply access the words or skills that we require. To begin with, it took me hours to learn a new language. In the end, minutes.'

Jeanette's cat strolled in, impatiently rubbing it's back across her legs. She ignored it.

'Do you know Latin?'

'Latin? I learnt it from an elderly priest. I could speak it fluently, along with ancient Greek, Gujarati from northern India, Cantonese, Turkish Kabardian. I could speak thirty-six languages in all, along with a number of dialects.'

Jeanette seemed surprised. 'So many? I never suspected. You could be a translator for any number of companies all over the world or even the UN, preventing disagreements between countries through lack of communication. Instead, you work in dead-end jobs helping no one. Why?'

'Because of what happened to Sharon. I couldn't bring myself to continue when she died.'

'I don't understand. Are you using my little girl's death as an excuse to be a failure? How selfish of you.'

I turned from the shelf to face the elderly woman. The setting sun cast a dull, rosy glow over everything.

'I…I killed her. I killed your Sharon and I can't forgive myself, even after all these years. That's why I despise myself.'

A shocked Jeanette stared at me, her eyes wide open. Then she slumped into her chair, holding her chest. Oh hell. I knew I shouldn't have said anything.

'In my bag. GTN,' she gasped.

I rushed to help her, passing the angina spray. Despite the disgust she must have felt for me, I couldn't bear to see her suffer.

A few minutes later, her breathing slowed. I was sitting again, staring at the cold coffee and half-nibbled biscuit. Although I asked if I should call the ambulance, she said no. She was fine again. It was a regular problem she had.

After some minutes, she felt up to resuming. 'I don't understand. Sharon was hit by a drunken businessman. He didn't even know his own name when he was dragged from the car. You had nothing to do with it.'

'I'd asked Sharon to buy some sweets with my pocket money. She was killed crossing the road. Don't you see?'

Jeanette stood up to cross the room. She cradled me in her arms. 'Oh, my poor child. It was the driver, only the driver. For years I blamed myself until I realised the truth.'

I looked up, wiping my tears away. 'You?'

'Sharon preferred to shop on our side of the road but I didn't like him for some long-forgotten reason. I made her promise to always go to Faulkner's over the road. I can understand that guilt, Kerry. I remember you weren't allowed to go to the funeral, as you were too young. If only you'd told someone how you felt… Now after all those wasted years, you should start to use your language skills again. Sharon would want you to and…so would I.'

She smiled at me tenderly just as Sharon did when she'd spoken to calm me down. We sat quietly for a while.

'Do you feel up to learning some French? My mother was from Brittany. She taught me, yet this ancient brain has probably forgotten it all.'

'You want me to learn French from you? I'll…I'll try. It's been so long and the mental blocks I set up…'

Closing my eyes, I felt the years melt away as Sharon's soft voice whispered to me. It was how I tuned into other brains. At first there was a void, so I delved deeper into my own mind. Suddenly I was able to converse in French. My vocabulary was limited, but tenses, adverbs were there, as well as something else. Something not quite right. I made a guttural miaowing sound, causing the cat to scurry into a corner.

'Tibbles is very hungry, Jeanette. I told him to be patient. I wasn't very polite, I'm afraid.'

'You speak cat? My goodness. Could you read my mind?'

'Only your language knowledge. Your French is quite advanced, actually. Thank you for allowing me to realise what I have to do with my life, now. But first, I think I have some explaining to do with my mother. Perhaps we can build a relationship after all.'

'Phone her now, sweetheart, and invite her for tea. It'll have to be takeaway, I'm afraid. Looks like the three of us have some planning to do.'

*

Six weeks later, having slimmed down considerably, I had a job with the United Nations. It wasn't difficult when I could speak the same language of anyone within the same room. I had to pretend a lot and never explained the reason for my linguistic skills.

*

I guess that you'll expect this story to end on some romantic, fairy tale note.

People, despite their denials and claims to the contrary, would love it if they found out that I'm now married to a Finnish diplomat and that we work together to make the world a better place. Possibly you'll even smile if I were to confess that our twin daughters said their first words of Portuguese today.

Happily ever after?

Who the hell knows?

This is just a story. Right? And if you believe that fiction is purely the expression of some writer's fertile imaginings, then I would suggest you stop reading now while happily ever after still exists as a possibility in your cosy little life.

However, if you are one of those people who believes in the possibility that truth can sometimes be veiled with fiction, then please read on. Remember, I did warn you, though.

*

I…I have another confession to make…When Jeanette asked if I could read her mind, I lied. Obviously, my innate abilities had been refined since I was eight. Every facet of her memory was open to my thoughts.

In fact, I've been developing my telepathic skills to the point that while you've been reading about me and my life, I've been learning about yours.

It's a very subtle link, yet now I'm aware of you.

That's right!

You!

Nothing too dramatic, mind: your name, where you live, what you ate for dinner, the last time you made love (which, I must agree, was pretty disappointing). So, nothing too deep, then. My telepathy does have its limits.

Nevertheless, I can sense your mouth drying and your heart beating faster, just like watching a horror film when the pretty teenager realises she's not alone.

Please don't glance to your side as though you felt someone move with your peripheral vision. I'm the intruder whom you'll never, ever catch.

Your secrets are safe…for now. I'm simply interested in who else is out there and what skills you might possess so that we might use them together to help this planet of ours. I'm not certain how long it will take before I visit you. It might be tomorrow…or one day next year… or never.

All I ask is that you be ready when I arrive. And once I do, you'll sense that I'm there. I'll be that woman watching you from across the street or sitting opposite you on the train. You'll be a little apprehensive, of course, but you'll feel secure because there are other people there to save you, surrounding you, ready to protect you. It's a natural reaction.

And then you'll hear me in your mind: the softest kiss caressing your thoughts and memories, and you'll realise how vulnerable you are.

Shushhh…

The Dating Game

'Jasmine Pownall, you are one gorgeous woman.'

The mirror didn't agree and on reflection, neither did I. Still, the fantasy was fine while it lasted and I'd done the best I could with what I had. The cluster of freckles still showed, my nose hadn't shrunk and my hair still looked like a kookaburra's nest despite yesterday's visit to the hairdresser.

Still, I was ready to hit the town in search of love. I was armed with the new app for meeting others in search of a meaningful relationship. Everyone said it was the latest thing in the technological dating game. Well, by everyone, I meant my two closest girlfriends. I was willing to try it. Lately, my love life had been a few disasters in between a lot of nights in watching box sets with my cat, Misty. Despite needing someone in my life, how would I find that ideal man?

The Loveaman app promised the solution. It was apparently inspired by the Pokeymon thingy I'd heard about where little animals appearing in real places. I took out my phone to check out the screen. Eight little male characters stared back at me, waiting. From time to time, they'd wave and stupidly I found myself waving back.

Each of them was a chosen potential match based on all the data I'd programmed in. They were local and expecting me to search for them today. All I had to do was wander around the streets of our large town and when I saw one of the cartoon men on my phone, I'd follow it to the real thing and we'd meet up in person. Simple. The idea behind it was that the game of searching for your perfect man was more romantic than turning up at a prearranged rendezvous.

I took a final wistful look in the mirror. My blouse was demure yet colourful, my plain red skirt was freshly ironed and the red leather Jimmy Choos that I'd treated myself to last year were clean and made me feel special even if I was still self-conscious about my appearance. First impressions count, my mum always said. Love comes later.

I sighed. 'Wish me luck, Misty,' I said before leaving my homely unit. Outwardly, I tried to smile and seem confident but inside I felt scared as hell.

Minutes later, I was walking towards Newton Valley's main street, constantly glancing at the phone screen in front of me. All I could see were real buildings, cars and people. Then, in the distance, I saw one of my cartoon guys waving at me. I clicked on his image.

'So, you're Jake? Real estate manager. Age, thirty-one,' I said, pensively.

A passing couple stared at me. Memo to self: don't talk out loud, Jasmine.

I checked out his details by clicking on his image as I followed it across two intersections and into a building. Cartoon Jake was smartly dressed. The app said that the real men would dress like their avatars, so things were looking fine. First impressions: he must take care of his appearance.

We were in a department store. I followed cartoon Jake up an escalator. Thinking the real Jake must be close, I began checking out the men I saw. A moment later, I saw him going through a door and made a move to follow him. Another man went in too. Woops. Realising I was about to enter the Gents, I veered away, somewhat embarrassed. I waited outside instead.

When Jake came out, I realised something wasn't quite right with him. He noticed too, surreptitiously rearranging his hairpiece. I decided then and there, Jake wasn't the man I thought he was and returned to the lower floor and most of the shops. Immediately, another cartoon figure appeared, beckoning me to follow it across the street to the hotel. The app told me this one was Marcus. Hopefully, he had all his own hair.

The real Marcus was in the foyer, complete with open shirt and medallion. Great. Before I could retreat, he held his phone up towards me and smiled a very toothy smile before stroking his moustache.

'Jasmine, I presume?'

I nodded, noticing that there was a cartoon avatar of me on his phone. Apparently, he'd been recently attacked by Aftershave Man, as he reeked of it. I recognised the pong. Sold by the litre at the local dollar shop.

'Shall we have a coffee in the café upstairs? Get to know one another? We can split the bill.'

Before I could think of an excuse, I found myself ushered into a lift. Talk about pushy.

'Actually, Jasmine, we should skip the refreshments and go straight to the room I've booked,' he suggested, before forcing me into a corner of the elevator. He leant across to kiss me, fumbling at my top button as he did so.

'In your dreams, mister,' I replied, as he doubled up on the floor. Exiting the elevator, I called back loudly enough to be heard by the hotel patrons and the girl on reception, 'Could I suggest a cold shower?'

I checked out my app and deleted Marcus from my list of suitors. His avatar was also doubled up on the floor before it winked out of existence. The app was more realistic than I thought.

Surely the third guy couldn't be as bad. The app had cost me a packet, latest system or not, and I wasn't about to throw that money away. I headed up the street towards the business area, and the man whose profile I thought to be the most promising: Tom Knighton.

It wasn't that his details on Loveaman said he was the CEO of a logistics firm, as much as the in-depth description of his sensitive, poetry-loving nature and his love for Siamese cats like my Misty. If he was a cat lover, he couldn't be bad, at least according to Mum. Unlike most of her advice, I agreed with her about that.

I scanned the busy streets with my phone held up in front. As lots of busy people wandered by, I noticed a cartoon man appear from behind a bus. It waved frantically before gesturing for me to cross the street. Although the lights took ages, the little man waited for me until I was near, then scurried into the front door of a large, imposing office block.

On the list of companies, I found Tom's company name on the third floor. The avatar was by the lift.

'Your boss had better be worth it,' I said to the little man on my phone. As no one else could see my app, I had another few strange looks and a smile from a twenty-something secretary doing her brunch run.

'Loveaman?' she asked as we both entered the elevator.

'Yes.' I showed her the app and the little guy apparently standing in a corner. 'Know him?' I asked, punching up his name.

Her smile faded as she glanced at my long, wavy hair. 'Good luck,' the attractive blonde replied.

I walked briskly into the reception area for Tom's firm, remembering to look as confident as I could. Having introduced myself to the desk attendant, I took a seat to wait for my possible future boyfriend. He was already aware of my name and that I was coming from Loveaman. The arrangement with all my potential dates is that today was a special meeting day and, even if they were working, they'd find time to get to know me.

To the receptionist, I was simply a client. I moved the phone around the room to see if little Tom was here with me. He was.

A moment later, I was told I could enter his office. He was typing on his computer.

'Hi. I'm Jasmine. Pleased to…' As I spoke, he looked up and his eyes opened wide in anger.

'You're a ginger.'

I adopted a more confrontational stance, hands on hips. 'Yes, I'm a ginger. So what?'

I noticed a framed photo on his desk and managed to examine it quickly before he realised it was there. He flipped it onto the desk.

'I hate gingers. I told the company that on my application. Clear off.'

'Gladly.' I stormed out of the office into the hall before stopping in the hall to catch my breath.

The nerve of that pig. For one terrifying moment I was back in school, listening to the taunts about my hair colour. Ginger Nut they called me, making reference to the hard biscuits everyone knew, as well as to my belligerent attitude.

Leaving the building, I was still seething with anger. Worse still was the photo on his desk: him and a woman with 'To My Darling Husband' written on it. In the past, they might have called him a cad. The words that I was now thinking of were much less polite. Not only had the man lied about being single, I thought I'd seen his wife somewhere recently.

All those years in school I'd had an attitude problem and being nicknamed a ginger because of my burnished copper hair hadn't helped. Just hearing that demeaning name once more still had me seething, my more passive older self struggling to cope.

I took out my phone, ready to delete Mr Two-timing Tom from my life forever, but was distracted by one of my other possible suitors appearing on the screen. I stopped. What should I do? My first three meetings were catastrophes. Should I persevere on my dating game? A part of me heard a truck horn sound but I dismissed it, too intent on my dilemma. Big mistake.

Suddenly I felt myself hurled through the air then crashing to the hard pavement. What the…? What was happening? I heard a man groaning from my side then hands releasing me from their grasp.

'Lady, what were you thinking?' yelled a voice in my ear.

I struggled to sit up, understanding that we were on the side of a road with bystanders gathering around. Traffic was roaring by. Whoever had sent me flying had saved me. I must have been stopped in the middle of the road, distracted by that stupid app. My phone was on the ground, obviously thrown from my hand.

'I'm sorry,' I stammered, only now realising that my knight in shining armour had cushioned my fall with his own body and that he was still partially underneath me. How embarrassing.

Some people helped me to struggle to my feet while others helped him up, praising his actions. We stood there, facing one another; the woman too preoccupied with some brainless game and the man who risked his own life to save her.

I thanked him profusely, expecting a well deserved telling-off.

Instead he responded with a question. 'Didn't you used to be Jasmine Pownall?'

'Yes…actually, I still am.' I held my ring finger up to prove it. So he knew me, though I couldn't remember him. Me and my rubbish memory for faces.

'Flynn Western? From school?' he said.

My mouth opened. Four-eyes Flynn: the only guy who didn't call me Ginger, mainly because he had his own bullying problems. No wonder I hadn't recognised him. When I'd last seen him, he was a scrawny little boy, even though he was eighteen at the time. Now he looked as though he was ready to play footy with the local premier league team. Obviously, a late developer.

I touched the bridge of my nose, giving him a quizzical look.

'Yeah. I wear contacts now. Still a computer geek. Still no luck with the ladies. I've concluded that no one likes a geek, even when he's not wearing specs.' He dusted off his casual clothes, wincing as he touched his elbow. Clearly, he'd suffered the brunt of the fall when he saved me.

Someone passed my phone back to me. I was tempted to throw it in the bin. It had almost got me killed. No, that was wrong. I…had almost got myself killed, believing that I had the latest gimmick to find Mr Right.

I began to leave, having remembered where I'd seen Two-timing Tom's wife yesterday. Perhaps he didn't like gingers, although I was certain his wife would dislike the news of her husband's attempted cheating even more. Then what? Home to Misty and another box set of shows?

I stopped before walking back to Flynn. Feeling a little scared, I kissed him. 'I always wanted to do that at school. You stood up for me when no one else did.'

As he didn't object, I kissed him again.

'What was the second one for?' he said.

'Because you saved my life and…and I wanted to. I've been using this Loveaman app and…'

He laughed. 'That daft thing. I wrote the programme for it years ago before selling it on. It was only later I realised it doesn't work.'

'It doesn't work? I just purchased it. What's the problem?'

'Oh, the app is fine. It's the personal data input. People lie, so you could end up chasing the wrong guy. I was too nerdy to understand that until later.'

I thought for a moment about that. So much for Loveaman. I stared at the pavement for a moment. My day of romance was finished.

Or…perhaps not.

'Flynn. I wonder if you're busy for the rest of the day. Lunch? Perhaps dinner? It's…it's the least I can do for stopping me being killed.'

He grinned. 'That sounds great. What about your other so-called dates, though?'

'I'm not bothered but I will keep the app for a few minutes longer. I'd like to detour via my hairdresser.'

I remembered where I'd seen Tom's wife. She owned the shop. Once I'd shown her Tom's profile, my ginger nut revenge would be complete. What's more, Flynn might even be able to do an app for wives to check up on cheating hubbies?

He reached out to take my hand. Sometimes the old-fashioned way of meeting that special man was much more fun than modern methods. My own dating game was just beginning to become interesting.

My Superhero Dad

I looked down at the neatly written pages in Brendan's English book. It wasn't the first time I'd read this essay, though it was still emotional. The class had been asked to write a page on the subject 'If my dad were a superhero, who would he be?'

It was his teacher who'd suggested I read it. She'd simply said. 'Brendan's struggling in class, Mrs Peters. Perhaps this might be the reason.'

Brendan had always found academic subjects difficult. He was great at art and sport, though. Nevertheless, Jim and I were so proud of him.

I began to read. The truth was, I knew it by heart, spelling mistakes and all. So did Jim. It had been one of those special moments in all our lives.

Now, on Father's Day, it seemed right to read it again.

If my dad was a superhero, he wood be the Unvisible Man. Whenever the baddies come looking for him they'd search everywhere but they'd never find him 'cause he'd be sumwhere else like down the pub with his mates or playing gulf or working till it was two late for anyone to see him, especially me and Mum. Unvisible people can't be seen but they can't see portant stuff either like if their children want to play or get help with there homework or just to talk…bout nuthin. Just talk.

My dad is a good superhero cause he works hard for me and Mum to get muney and stuff like that. He has a secret identidy two like all superheros where he's a normal dad. The trouble is he likes to stay Unvisible. And that makes me sad.

Brendan Peters aged nine.

I put the book down. On that day long ago, I could remember sobbing for hours. Somehow through the years since we'd married, life had changed and us along with it. Jim's promotion at work. My own involvement with friends. The fact was that we'd grown apart and Brendan wasn't coping.

I'd decided to make Jim read it that night. As usual, Brendan was asleep when Jim arrived home for dinner. I'd waited until he was finished before showing him the book. At first he'd told me he had a presentation to finalise. He never did finish that presentation. He'd put in his resignation the day after. 'Priorities,' he'd told his boss. After much arguing and debate, he'd decided to stay but without the impossibly long hours. He'd given up golf and visits to the pub.

That weekend, he and Brendan had spent the day getting to know one another again. They'd gone to play tennis, although there was much more talking than playing. Brendan came home with a smile for the first time in months. So did Jim. When he'd suggested a holiday to Bali the following month, I'd told him I was too busy to take time off work. I'd conceded after ten minutes of gentle persuasion from my two men and that's when life suddenly improved for all of us.

'Reading that silly essay, Mum?'

I turned. There was Brendan in the doorway. Little Brendan wasn't so little any longer.

'Put it down, please. We need you outside. Dad and I are challenging your grandchildren to a game of footie. Our annual Father's Day grudge match.'

I laughed. 'Referee again?'

As I left, there was a noise behind me. I ignored it. After all, the Unvisible Man had vanished thirty years ago. We'd never seen him again but, then again, being unvisible, we never would.

Serves You Right

Andrea, the assistant manager at Hildon's Super Pharmacy, knocked on her boss's door before entering.

'About time. Do you have the monthly sales figures yet?' said the manageress. She was trying to read a magazine.

'Put them on your desk first thing. Although I should point out that it's your job to prepare them, Mrs Taylor. I had to stay till ten o'clock.'

'Your job, Andrea, is to do whatever I tell you. Besides, you have to make up time for that regional conference you insisted on attending last week. Was the new regional manager there?'

'Yes, Mrs Taylor. He was…'

'Don't want to hear about it. Just so long as he lets me run my store my way and doesn't interfere. One other thing: don't suppose you've seen my reading glasses? No? I'm sure they were here this morning.' She resumed squinting at the latest copy of *La Belle Soirée* fashion magazine then looked up. 'Is that all? If not, you're dismissed.'

'Sorry, there was one thing. You might want to know that someone looking exactly like your husband just came into the store. I thought you told him never to come here again.'

Janet Taylor threw her paperwork down. 'That little worm.' She glanced across at the remnants of the photo of Mr Taylor that was pinned to a dart board.

'What are you going to do?'

'Teach him a lesson he'll never forget.' She stood up, hands gripping her desk. 'Where are my glasses?'

'You're wearing them.'

'Not these, you idiot. I want my reading glasses. Find them and bring them to the Security office. Where was he? What was he wearing? How dare he set foot in my store again after what he did to me.'

'Wandering around Aisle 2. And he had a bright red-checked shirt on, like the one on that photo.' Andrea pointed to the one on the board.

Janet was livid. Slamming the door behind her, she marched down the corridor. 'Get out of my way,' she shouted at some cleaner whose name she didn't know and didn't care about anyway.

Entering the video room, she went to the bank of screens that monitored the two floors of her store. 'Move, Christine,' she instructed the pretty twenty-something woman watching diligently. Janet strained to see her soon to be ex-husband on the screens. Without her glasses, it was very blurry. 'Red shirt, red shirt,' she muttered. 'Where are you hiding, you slimy slug?'

'Red shirt, Mrs Taylor? Is that him? He's the only red shirt in the store,' said Christine, trying to be helpful. She was still on probation and was keen to make a good impression on her new boss.

'Yes, it must be. Pass me the microphone. Now.'

Janet's anger towards her husband was apparent to all the staff. She'd been in a foul temper for weeks, ever since he'd refused to take her back and had filed for divorce. She ignored the fact that she'd left him for a young Polish rep whom she'd fallen in love with. Unfortunately, their relationship didn't last long, so she'd assumed that Mr Taylor would take her back. He didn't. Now there was war.

'Treat me like dirt, will you?' She switched on the announcement system. 'Could a staff member please check if we have any Viagra for the gentleman in the red-checked shirt? He's waiting near the checkouts.'

Immediately she could see dozens of customers and staff turning towards the middle-aged man standing there.

She flipped the microphone switch to off. 'That'll teach you to dump me,' she cackled as she rubbed her hands with glee. She could see people laughing on the screens.

The Security door buzzed then opened. Andrea entered.

'What have you done? You can't embarrass people like that.'

'I can do whatever I want, lady. I'm your manager. Don't ever question me again. Now, where are those glasses? I want to see the expression on his smug little face. I want to relish this moment.'

'I couldn't find them.'

'Doesn't matter. I'll rerun this later. In slow motion.'

In the corner of the room, Christine kept her head down.

Janet returned to the screen. She had another idea. 'Staff announcement. The man in the red shirt is still waiting for his Viagra. Also, he requires assistance in finding medication for halitosis. That's bad breath for any of the staff who are unaware of what halitosis means. Almost forgot: he needs antibiotics for a highly infectious skin problem he caught from a massage parlour.'

By now, most customers in the store were gathered around the red-shirted man. They moved further away after the last announcement.

Janet turned the switch to off again. 'Lovely,' she said, smiling. At that point, she opened her phone to press speed dial. 'Did you enjoy that, you useless piece of trash?' she yelled.

'Enjoy what, Janet?' Her husband's voice was so calm. It always made Janet more angry and he knew it.

Janet stared at the screen. The man wasn't on the phone. What was happening?

'Don't pretend. I've embarrassed you, admit it. I can see you, in my store, Mark.'

'I'm on the golf course, not that it's any of your business. Sounds like you've been drinking again, Janet. Now please excuse me. It's my putt. Goodbye.'

'But…but. If you're there, who's here? Oh hell. It's not Mark down there.'

Janet rushed to the door. Insulting her husband was one thing. Insulting a member of the public was quite another. This required damage limitation, big time. If only she'd seen more clearly, she would have realised it wasn't Mark.

She hurried as fast as she could, down the stairs and across the expansive ground floor. Bad news. The crowds were still there. The good news was that meant he hadn't left to tweet or Facebook all about the incident to the cyberworld.

He was still standing in the same place when Janet arrived, out of breath.

'I'm the store manageress, sir. I must humbly apologise for this dreadful fiasco. Apparently one of our junior security personnel decided to have a silly prank at your expense. Thought you were one of her ex-boyfriends. I have already suspended her and will formally dismiss her within the hour. You have my word.'

Janet needed a sacrificial scapegoat and that Christine woman in Security would do nicely. Besides, she was far too attractive.

'Would you be kind enough to come with me so that I can offer some refreshment while I investigate this gross insult further.'

Turning to the assemblage, Janet assumed her best manageress voice. 'Nothing to see here, ladies and gentlemen. A misunderstanding. Hildon's would never insult any of our valued customers and I must formerly apologise to Mr...'

'Atkinson. Ron Atkinson.'

'Mr Atkinson. I'm extremely sorry.'

As the spectators began to disperse, she spied Andrea and summoned her, whispering as the two women walked in front of the seemingly bewildered victim, 'What made you possibly think that he was my husband, Andrea?'

'Don't blame me, Mrs Taylor. You're married to him and you thought he was Mark too. How was I to know what you planned to do?'

'That's true. But it's still your fault for not finding those glasses. I don't understand why I tolerate your incompetence. Now, get us some coffee and Danish from the shop across the way and bring them to your office. I need to sweet-talk him. Don't want him complaining to head office.'

'Why my office?'

'Because, you silly cow, there's a photo of a man in a red shirt on my dartboard. Duh!'

The manageress ushered Ron Atkinson into the tiny office. He was quite restrained, given the situation. Janet had already summoned Christine, who now stood there, wondering what was happening.

'Do you have anything to say for yourself, young lady? No, of course not. Your behaviour was appalling. You're dismissed. No notice and definitely no references.'

'But Mrs Taylor. I didn't do nothing. It was…'

'Don't want to hear it now. Shut up and clear off. Now,' screamed Janet.

Christine burst into tears before running out.

'I'm sorry that you had to witness that, Mr Atkinson. No remorse at all. Disgusting. Nevertheless, you can see how seriously I take that sort of unforgivable behaviour.'

'I'd hate to think that poor girl lost her job over something so minor. In a way, I found it amusing – her comments, I mean.'

'That's so understanding but standards need to be maintained. Any one insulting a customer must be sacked.'

'Anyone?'

'Of course.'

Andrea returned at that moment with the peace offering. She offered the food and drink to Ron and her boss.

'Was that Christine I saw outside? She seemed very upset.'

'Don't worry your head about it, Andrea. Senior management decision.'

As they ate and sipped their drinks, Ron began chatting to Janet. He seemed more relaxed. Janet was also relaxing. Crisis averted.

Suddenly he asked something that caught her off-guard. 'So where did the young lady make her announcement?'

'Er…the Security office, I suppose.'

'Might I see this office?'

'I guess, although there's nothing to see. Simply a load of monitors.'

'Humour me, Mrs Taylor. Please.'

Janet was beginning to feel a little uncomfortable. Nevertheless, what harm could it do? The three of them made their way to the room down the corridor.

Once inside, Ron continued to show a more assertive side. 'So Christine would have been watching me on these screens and then using this microphone?'

Janet answered, 'I suppose…'

'And her activities would have been recorded by that camera.' He pointed.

'What…what camera?' She could see it now, its little red light flashing.

'Shame on you, Mrs Taylor. Not knowing your own store's monitoring system. Let's see now. That's the playback button.'

'Oh, you can't touch that, Mr Atkinson. That's for staff only. Confidentiality.'

'Don't worry you little head, Mrs Taylor. I am staff. I'm your new regional manager.'

'Oh. But I thought…' She turned to Andrea in anger. 'You knew who he was all the time. Why didn't you say?'

Andrea shrugged. An angry Janet made a move towards her but stopped short when Ron pressed the rewind button to a time stamp when he'd entered the store.

'Temper, temper, Mrs Taylor. Let's simply relax and watch the show. I don't suppose you have any popcorn?'

Janet didn't need to watch. She knew she was finished. It all made sense now: the missing glasses, the red-checked shirt that was identical to the one on the dartboard photo, plus her own stupid temper. She'd been set up by her assistant manager and she'd walked right into it.

Ron pressed pause, leaving Janet to gaze at herself on the screen, microphone in hand.

'Mrs Taylor? I believe your exact words were that anyone insulting a customer should be sacked.'

'But you weren't a customer,' Janet responded weakly. It wasn't the best response.

'Andrea, I'm appointing you manager. Could you please have someone escort Mrs Taylor from the premises after she clears her desk. I'll apologise to Christine personally. I'm certain we can find a permanent position for her now. But first of all, I have to change out of this ridiculous red shirt you gave me yesterday. It might suit your new boyfriend, but it's not my style.'

'Boyfriend? Andrea actually has a boyfriend?' Janet asked.

'Yes, I met him yesterday.' Ron said, innocently. 'A pleasant man, likes golf. Mark someone or other.'

The Collector of Nothings

'He's obsessed, Alicia.'

'Shane? What with?'

'His horrible mania for collecting, that's what,' Kerry said, slamming the drawer closed.

Although I'd only arrived this morning, Kerry couldn't keep her anger under control any longer. She fought to stop from bursting into tears and, being her big sister, it was important to listen to her and guide her through life's little problems. In Kerry's case, she'd had more than her share of those.

Even though I hadn't been around for the eight months since the so-called fairy tale wedding, to see her as upset as this was hardly surprising. I had warned her about him but no, she knew best and no amount of talking to her had changed her mind.

I decided not to play the I told-you-so card.

'Surely it can't be that bad, Kerry. We all have our little idiosyncrasies. I remember you used to collect anything Barbie when you were younger. So what is Shane so obsessed with anyway?'

'That's just it. He spends all his spare time searching for nothings.'

'Sorry. Don't you mean "nothing"? And how can anyone collect nothing anyway?'

She stifled a sob, dabbed her eyes and walked into the hallway. 'No. I did mean nothings. Perhaps it's easier if I show you. Follow me. He's built a special display room out back.'

I'd always been there for her to talk to, especially in the early years when she needed me most, after Mum ran off. It had broken Kerry's heart. To begin with, Dad didn't mind me being there for her, because he was so busy working and coping with the divorce. However, as

Kerry became older, he resented us being so close. When Kerry had married, she thought she had someone else to confide in, shutting me out. A shame really. Now that things were going wrong with their marriage, she wanted me back in her life and I was only too happy to be there for her once more.

'In here,' she gestured, opening an old wooden door. She closed it carefully behind us.

'Kerry? Can we have the lights on?'

'Don't need them. You'll see in a moment.'

Suddenly a group of twinkling lights appeared, before exploding into a cavalcade of colours. The room came alive, although it wasn't a room since there were no walls or ceiling, just open space in every direction. I realised that included the floor. We were suspended on nothing at all.

'Wh-what the…'

'Shane's special place. You see, Shane's not an ordinary man. He has certain…skills. It's amazing what a little Tesseract technology can do and Shane's great with a hammer and power drill. This place… It's different, isn't it? Shane says it needs to be outside normal reality otherwise he couldn't keep his collection here.'

I thought she didn't approve of his obsession but now she seemed elated. Strange. I thought about this for an instant before dismissing the inconsistency. Kerry had always been changeable in her moods. At that moment, a rainbow-coloured cat jumped onto a table by the door. Its radioactive purr was much louder than any cat I'd heard.

'Hi, Genesis. Lovely to see you.'

Kerry reached to stroke him as his fur phased through various hues. 'Shane found him for me in an alternative dimension. He's one of our collection: an imaginary number corresponding to the square root of minus one. Cute, isn't he?'

'Rubbish, Kerry. He's simply a strange-coloured…koala?'

Her pet had changed before my eyes. What was he? What was this room anyway? Was I hallucinating?

'He's just playing around, enjoying being real for a while. I can't understand how lonely it must be to be a number that doesn't exist, can you?'

I didn't answer. Instead, I looked around. The room was piled high with strange objects as well as familiar furnishings. An empty skyscraper rose so high I couldn't see the top of it.

'Shane's been busy collecting for ages. His prize possessions are over here. It's only a couple of parsecs away. Come on. You'll love them.'

I tried to recall how far a parsec was. Three light years? Twenty trillion miles? Had my sister finally lost all reason?'

'Oh, don't panic. The rules of time and space don't apply here, sis. Those lights we saw? A mixture of quarks and quanta. So small we can't normally see them but here it's all different. There's a black hole around somewhere and that is really, really huge. Oh, there it is.' She pointed to a dark spot sucking in light. 'They'll all just different versions of nothings.'

Once we reached a large mahogany cabinet, Kerry opened a drawer to remove an ancient parchment. I noticed something scuttle across the non-existent floor from the corner of my eye.

'What was that?' I asked, feeling a little afraid.

Although Kerry seemed more relaxed than I'd ever seen her, I was becoming edgy. There was something here that set my teeth on edge…

'Oh, it's nothing,' she laughed. 'Some people call them boogie-men, pookas or pixies. Lots of names for something that doesn't exist.'

'Doesn't exist? I saw one.'

'Did you? Or did you think you did? Here, the make-believe can become real.'

I shuddered. Despite the fascination of this magical room, this was becoming too terrifying.

'Did you know the number zero was invented by ancient Indian mathematicians?' She showed me the faded parchment. 'Here's the first time it was written down; the very first time. Shane collected it. The

Romans never had a symbol for nothing. Only Xs and Vs and such,' she said as she opened another box. 'This is my favourite. Absolute zero. Minus 273 degrees Celsius, or 0 degrees Kelvin: the coldest temperature possible where nothing, not even electrons, can move.'

There were soft murmurs from the air around me, the replies of guilty children when asked what they were doing, the remains of a relationship when love had gone, cries of emptiness. zilch, diddly-squat and bugger-all caressed the non-existent walls. My skin felt as cold as that absolute zero I had just seen.

'Can we leave now, Kerry? Which way is out?'

'Surely you're not afraid, Alicia. There's so much more to see. Every song about nothing is crammed into this tiny box. Remember "All or Nothing at All", my loving sister? You used to sing it to me every bloody night while I was trying to sleep.'

'Kerry, how can you say that? I was only thinking of you, sweetheart. Trying to help you realise that you weren't alone and Mother didn't abandon you.'

At that moment, Shane seemed to appear from nowhen, some sidereal plane of existence next to our own. I realised then that it was a trap…for me. All of this nonsense about being afraid of Shane's obsession was only a trick to bring me into this fantastical room. I tried to run, only to find myself entangled by zeros, linked together in a chain that was forever-long.

'Let me go,' I shouted. They didn't. 'Why are you doing this, Kerry? I've always been there, whenever you needed me. Nothing was too much.'

Kerry and Shane faced me, hand in hand as I struggled against my confines. They only grew tighter.

Shane kissed my sister on the cheek as she smiled for the first time since I could remember. 'She looks so human, Kerry. Even seeing the universe as I have, I could never quite believe your explanation of the torment she put you through – the older sister who almost destroyed your life. All of those years convincing you to reject everyone else in your life apart from her. How does it feel to have her out of your life at last?'

'Satisfying, my dearest Shane. Very satisfying.'

I glared at the pair of them. So smug. So perfect. Despite me straining with all of my strength, I was helpless. I ground my teeth, spitting out a stream of vindictive swear words at her. How could she do this to me, the evil little whore? 'I'm your sister, you bitch,' I yelled, finally collapsing from the exertion.

'You were never that, Alicia. You were a parasitic creature from some netherworld that found a frightened girl, upset that her mother had left her. You took my childhood from me, jealously destroying all my friendships…until Shane came into my life. Gradually he showed me how to fight back, my regain my self-worth until I was able to make you leave me all those months ago.'

I hated her for that, hated her standing up to me, hated her thinking she could live a life without me by her side.

She wasn't finishing gloating yet. 'I thought I'd rid myself of you but you were still there, murmuring to me in my dreams, trying to break my resolve. Then Shane made this place, with a way to capture you and make sure you never bother me again. So I let myself need you, tricking you into entering this room where the tesseracts warped reality until even my imaginary sister could be real.'

'It's only fitting, Alicia,' Shane added. 'You're an ugly little nothing, a beast without a soul. So here, in our special place filled with nothings, you'll be right at home.'

Kerry blew a kiss in my direction. 'Goodbye, sweet sister of mine. I won't be seeing you again.'

As they walked through the door back to reality, the lights faded. I stared into the darkness, still breathing heavily, forcing myself to calm down, to conserve my energy, to plan my revenge for this betrayal. After all, Kerry and me, we're family. She'll come back for me. I'll be safe here until she does. I'm imaginary. I don't really exist. Nothing can hurt me.

Suddenly, there were sounds from behind: slithering, scampering, scratching sounds. I shuddered as they came closer. Slimy cold tongues began licking my skin. Fetid breath caressed my face. Then I heard a long-dead whisper.

'You're sooo wrong, Aliciaaa.' My eyes opened wide. 'Innn thisss place, weee nothings can hurt youuu. Nowww, ssshall weee beginnn?'